"We're married now," ... **would at least hug me** ...

"You don't want me to ... it to say, I'm a little...overstimulated."

"So you're turned on."

She looked in his eyes and— *Whoa.* The heat smoldering in their dark depths could have burned a hole through her dress. Her heart flip-flopped, making her pulse race and her mouth go dry.

"You want the truth?" he said.

She nodded.

He leaned in just a little closer. "I wanted everyone to leave the reception so I could lock the door, strip you naked and lick wedding cake off every inch of your body."

Oh, boy. "Every inch?"

He grinned. "Every inch. However," he added, "friends don't do that."

"Some friends do. And I'm pretty sure I read somewhere that we have to consummate the marriage to make it official and legally binding."

* * *

More Than a Convenient Bride is part of the series
Texas Cattleman's Club: After the Storm—
As a Texas town rebuilds, love heals all wounds...

* * *

If you're on Twitter,
tell us what you think of Harlequin Desire!
#harlequindesire

Dear Reader,

Natural disasters suck. Even on a small scale. Recently in the Metro Detroit area, where I've lived my entire life, we had torrential rains that caused flooding. Some areas were several feet underwater. The property damage was mind-boggling. My poor car drowned in two feet of water in the parking lot of the local Costco. Businesses were forced to close their doors, and basements flooded with sewage-tainted rainwater, making thousands of homes uninhabitable. Areas went without power for days—and in some cases weeks—afterward.

Needless to say it gave me an interesting perspective while writing Luc and Julie's story. Best-friends-to-lovers stories have always been my favorite. Throw in a natural disaster, irresistible sexual attraction and an ex-fiancée, and it makes for one heck of a story. I hope you enjoy their journey as much as I loved writing it.

Michelle

MORE THAN A CONVENIENT BRIDE

——

MICHELLE CELMER

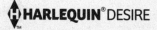

Special thanks and acknowledgment
are given to Michelle Celmer for her
contribution to the Texas Cattleman's Club:
After the Storm miniseries.

ISBN-13: 978-0-373-73373-6

More Than a Convenient Bride

Recycling programs
for this product may
not exist in your area.

Printed in U.S.A.

www.Harlequin.com

Michelle Celmer is a bestselling author of more than thirty books. When she's not writing, she likes to spend time with her husband, kids, grandchildren and a menagerie of animals.

Michelle loves to hear from readers. Visit her website, michellecelmer.com, like her on Facebook or write her at PO Box 300, Clawson, MI 48017.

Books by Michelle Celmer

HARLEQUIN DESIRE

The Nanny Bombshell
Princess in the Making

Black Gold Billionaires
The Tycoon's Paternity Agenda
One Month with the Magnate
A Clandestine Corporate Affair
Much More Than a Mistress

The Caroselli Inheritance
Caroselli's Christmas Baby
Caroselli's Baby Chase
Caroselli's Accidental Heir

The Texas Cattleman's Club: After the Storm
More Than a Convenient Bride

Visit the Author Profile page
at Harlequin.com for more titles.

To Best Friends

One

Julie Kingston stood and waited in the crowd, her heart overflowing with pride as her best friend and colleague, Lucas Wakefield, prepared to cut the ribbon marking the opening of the new, state-of-the-art Wakefield Clinic. It seemed as though the entire town of Royal, Texas, had shown up to mark the occasion.

The town's original free clinic once stood directly in the path of the F5 tornado that had ripped through Royal last October. In the blink of an eye, all that had remained of the structure was the concrete foundation. Patients from all over the surrounding counties had lost an important lifeline in the community.

Lucas, who had been a regular volunteer there despite his duties as chief of surgery at Royal Memorial Hospital, hadn't hesitated to donate the money to rebuild, using some of the proceeds from the sales and licensing of surgical equipment he'd invented several years ago.

Humble as he was for a multimillionaire, he'd intended to keep his identity as the donor a secret, but someone leaked the truth, and the news spread through Royal like wildfire. The town council had immediately wanted to rename the clinic in his honor. But of course

Luc had protested when he'd heard about plans for the Lucas Wakefield Clinic.

"This clinic doesn't belong to me," he'd told Julie when she'd tried to convince him that he was being ridiculous. "It belongs to the people."

"This is a huge deal," she'd argued time and again. "You donated millions of dollars."

He gave her his usual, what's-your-point shrug, as if he truly didn't understand the scope of his own good will. For a man of his wealth and breeding he lived a fairly simple life. "It was the right thing to do."

And that was Luc in a nutshell. He always did the right thing, constantly putting the well-being of others first. But finally, after much debate, and a whole lot of coercing from his mother, Elizabeth, Julie and his colleagues in the Texas Cattleman's Club, he relented, allowing the use of his last name only.

Julie smiled and shook her head as she thought back on it. Lucas was the most philanthropic, humble man she had ever known. And at times, the most stubborn, as well.

Luc looked out over the crowd, and when his eyes snagged on hers she flashed him a reassuring smile. Despite his dynamic presence, and easy way with his patients and coworkers, he despised being the center of attention.

To his left stood Stella Daniels, the town's acting mayor. To his right, Stella's new husband, Aaron Nichols, whose company R&N Builders rebuilt the clinic. In the six months since the storm, the town's recovery had been slow but steady, and now it seemed as if every week a new business would reopen or a family would move back into their home.

"I'm so proud," Elizabeth Wakefield said, dabbing away a tear with the corner of a handkerchief. Julie knelt beside the wheelchair Elizabeth had been forced to use since a botched surgery a decade ago left her paralyzed from the waist down. In the months since Julie came to Royal last October, Elizabeth had contracted a multitude of infections that led to numerous hospital stays, and she now required permanent, round-the-clock care from a registered nurse. Though she was a beautiful and proud woman, she looked every one of her sixty-eight years, and a recent hospital stay for viral pneumonia had left her weak and vulnerable. Originally Luc forbade her from attending the ribbon cutting, but she insisted she be there. After much debate, he eventually caved, and it was more than clear to Julie where he inherited his stubborn streak.

"You have every reason to be proud," Julie said, patting Elizabeth's frail arm. "You've raised your son to be an amazing man."

"I wish his father could be here. From the day Luc was born he insisted that his son was destined for great things. It still breaks my heart that he didn't live to see how right he was."

Julie took her trembling hand and gave it a gentle squeeze. "He knows."

The mayor completed her brief speech and handed Luc a pair of gold-plated scissors. With a quick swish of the blades the ribbon drifted to the freshly laid grass, and a round of applause erupted from the crowd. Luc's club brothers crowded around him to congratulate him and shake his hand, but Julie hung back, still clutching his mother's hand. Elizabeth looked proud but tired. The simplest of activities exhausted her.

"We should get you home," her nurse, Theresa, said.

Too sleepy to argue, Elizabeth nodded.

"Shall I call Luc over?" Julie asked. "So you can say goodbye?"

"Oh no, don't bother him. I'll see him at home later tonight."

Julie kissed her papery cheek and said goodbye, then joined her friends Beth Andrews and Megan Maguire several feet away.

"She doesn't look so good," Beth said as Theresa wheeled Luc's mother toward the parking lot to the van Luc had custom-built for her. When it came to taking care of his mother, he spared no expense.

A stab of sadness pierced Julie's heart. In the six months since she'd moved to Royal, Julie had come to consider Elizabeth a dear friend. She was the closest thing Julie had had to a mother since her own mother died giving birth to her sister, Jennifer. Her father waited to remarry until after she and her sister had left home, and though he dated, he'd never brought a woman home to meet his daughters. He traveled extensively, so they were raised by nannies and the other house staff. Homeschooled by tutors.

And when he was home? Well, she didn't like to think about that.

"I don't suppose you'll have any free time to volunteer this week," Megan said. "Just an hour or two? Someone left a cardboard box of three-week-old puppies on the doorstep. They need to be bottle-fed every hour or so and I'm ridiculously understaffed this week." Manager of the local animal shelter, she was known for taking in strays. Animals and humans alike. She had certainly gone out of her way to make Julie feel welcome when she arrived in Royal. Her significant other, as well as Beth's, were members of the Cattleman's Club with Luc.

It was shaping up to be a very busy week, but Julie could always make time to help a friend. And sadly, this would probably be the last time. "Of course," Julie said. "Just let me know when you need me."

Megan sighed with relief. "You're a lifesaver!"

They stood chatting for several minutes, before Julie heard a familiar voice say, "Good afternoon, ladies."

She turned as Luc joined them, smiling brightly to hide the deep feeling of sadness that seemed to radiate from the center of her bones. She could tell by the way he tugged at his tie that he was already irritable. No sense in making him feel even worse.

"It's a wonderful thing you've done," Megan told him, and Beth nodded in agreement.

"Thank you, ma'am," he said, pouring on the Texas charm. Though he was her boss, and they had never been more than friends—best friends, but just friends—that drawl sometimes gave her a warm feeling inside her bones.

"Can I give you a lift home?" he asked Julie. Her apartment was within walking distance from the clinic, and it was a sunny and pleasant day for a stroll, but she suspected he was looking for any excuse to leave.

"If you wouldn't mind," she said, playing along, noticing a look pass between Megan and Beth, as if they knew Luc was eager to escape.

"Good to see you ladies," he said, nodding cordially, that hint of Texas twang boosting his charm somewhere into the stratosphere.

Julie followed him to his car, his stride so much longer than hers she practically had to run to keep up.

"What's your rush," she said, though she already knew the answer.

"Damn," Luc muttered, pulling at his tie as if it were a noose. "Why does everyone have to make such a big deal about it?"

Seriously? "Because it *is* a big deal, doofus. You're a hero."

"It's not as if I built it with my own two hands," he said, using his key fob to unlock his Mercedes. "I just wrote out a check."

"A ridiculously enormous check," she reminded him as he opened the door for her. He'd also remained involved through the design stage and the construction process, to be sure that everything was built to his exact specifications. Whether he wanted to admit it or not, this was, in many ways, *his* clinic.

As they drove through town, sadness and regret leaked from every pore. In the six months she'd been here, Royal had become her haven. The US felt like more of a home to her now than her native South Africa, and now she had to leave. She had no idea where she would go, or what she would do, and she had little time to figure it out.

Silence filled the car, and as they pulled into the gated community where she was currently staying, Luc said, "You're awfully quiet. Would you like to talk about it?"

"Talk about what?" she asked, dreading the inevitable conversation. But Luc could always tell when she was upset. She could swear that sometimes he knew her better than she knew herself.

"Whatever is bothering you." He parked outside her condo and turned to her. "Did I do something to upset you?"

"No, of course not." She'd hoped to put this off a little while longer, so as not to dampen his special day, but there was so much concern in the depths of his eyes, it seemed only fair to tell him now.

"So, what is it?"

As her brain worked to find the appropriate words, tears burned the backs of her eyes. Maybe the parking lot wasn't the best place to do this.

"Can you come inside for a few minutes? We need to talk."

His brow furrowed, he killed the engine. "Of course. Is everything okay?"

No, not at all. "Let's talk inside."

Gentleman that he was, Luc took her keys as they reached her door and unlocked it for her. He didn't even do it consciously. It was just his way. His mother, born and bred in Georgia, was old-fashioned when it came to matters of social grace. He claimed that from the day he was born, she'd drilled him with proper Southern manners.

Whatever she'd done, it had worked. He was one of the most courteous men Julie had ever known. In all the time they had been friends and worked together, he'd never said a harsh word, or once raised his voice to her. Or to anyone else, for that matter. He had such a commanding presence, he never had to. People took one look at those piercing hazel eyes and that *GQ*-worthy physique, heard the deep baritone voice, and spontaneously bent to his will. Women especially.

As they stepped inside the apartment, afternoon sunshine and fresh spring air poured in through the partially open window in the living room. Luc shrugged out of his suit jacket and dropped like a lead weight onto the sofa, looking far too masculine for the floral printed chintz. The furniture, which was too formal and froofy for her taste, and not all that comfortable, either, came with the apartment. Expecting good news when she'd filed to renew her visa, she'd been tentatively window-shopping in her spare time for furniture more suited to her. She wouldn't be needing it now. Not here, anyway.

She wasn't even sure where she would live. Other than a few distant aunts and uncles, she had no family left in her hometown. And when her father had passed away, his wife, whom Julie never had the pleasure of meeting, sold off the entire estate before the body was cold.

Julie had so much to plan, and so little time to do it.

She set her purse on the coffee table and sat beside Luc, fisting her hands in her lap. There was nothing she hated more than giving good people bad news.

Luc unknotted his tie, tugged it off and tossed it over the sofa arm on top of his jacket. Relaxing back against the cushions he undid the top two buttons of his dress shirt. "Okay, let's hear it."

She took a deep breath, working up the nerve to tell him. "I heard back from immigration yesterday."

One brow rose in anticipation. "And?"

Just say it, Jules. "My application to renew my visa again was denied."

In a blur of navy blue Italian silk and white Egyptian cotton, Luc was on his feet. "*Denied*? You can't be serious."

Tears pricked the corners of her eyes. Now was not the time for a messy emotional display. She'd learned years ago that crying only made things worse. "According to your government I've overstayed my welcome. I have two weeks to pack up my things and get out of the US."

"How is that possible? You're on a humanitarian mission."

"Technically I'm on a work visa."

"I still don't see the problem. You're still my research assistant. Gainfully employed. What changed?"

"Remember how I told you that in college I attended several protests."

"I remember."

"Well, what I didn't tell you is that I was arrested a few times."

"Were you convicted?"

"No, but I was afraid that if I put it down on my application I would be denied."

"So you left it out?"

She bit her lip and nodded, feeling juvenile and ashamed for having lied in the first place. But she would have done almost anything to come to the US and help her best friend. Now that one serious lapse in judgment was coming back to bite her in the rear. "I screwed up. I thought that because the charges were dropped, and it was a peaceful political protest, it wouldn't matter anyway. I was wrong."

"There has to be something we can do," he said, pacing the oriental rug, brow deeply furrowed. "Maybe I could talk to someone. Pull some strings."

"The decision is final."

His chin tilted upward. "I can't accept that."

She rose from the sofa, touching his arm, stopping him in his tracks. "You don't have a choice. It's done."

He muttered a curse, one he wouldn't normally use in the presence of a female, and wrapped his arms around her, pulling her close. She rested her head against his chest, breathed in the scent of his after-shave. It wasn't often that they embraced this way, and she found herself dreading the moment he let go.

The stubble on his chin brushed her forehead as he spoke. "There has to be something we can do."

There was one thing, but it was too much to ask. Even of him. *Especially* of him. "At this point all I can do is accept it. And move on."

He held her at arm's length, and she could see the wheels in his head spinning. But this was one situation all his money and influence couldn't fix. "Where will you go?"

"South Africa for a while, until I can find another research assistant position. Maybe in Europe, or even Asia."

"I'll do whatever I can to help. I'll write such a glowing recommendation people will be clamoring to hire you."

The problem was, she didn't want to work for any-one else. She used to love moving from place to place, meeting new people and learning new cultures and customs. Now the only place she could imagine liv-ing was right here in Royal. It was the first place in her travels that had genuinely felt like home. The first place in her life really.

There had to be something she could do.

Two

Luc sat at the bar at the Cattleman's Club swirling a double Scotch, watching the amber liquid tornado along the sides of a crystal tumbler, still reeling from Julie's news. And wracking his brain for a way to fix this, to keep her here in Royal where she belonged. Where she wanted to be.

She was the only person in his life—aside from his mother—who truly understood him. Who knew what made him tick. In fact, there were times when he wondered if she knew him better than he knew himself. These past few months, with the stress of seeing his hometown devastated, she was the anchor that had kept him grounded. She had been there to support him during his mother's past two hospital stays, which seemed to stretch longer each time she was admitted. Julie sat with her on her breaks, read to her when she was too weak to hold a book in her own two hands. He never even had to ask for her help. She just seemed to sense when he needed her, and she was there.

Drew Farrell, a fellow club member, and the owner of Willowbrook Farms, slid onto the stool beside him at the bar. In blue jeans, worn boots and a dusty cowboy hat, he looked more like a ranch hand than a man responsible for breeding multiple Triple Crown–winning horses. And though he dealt regularly with an elite and prestigious clientele, he couldn't be more down-to-earth. He was that guy in town everyone liked. Well, everyone but his neighbor Beth Andrews, who, up until the storm, had it in for Drew. But now, by some strange twist of fate, they were engaged to be married.

The complicated nature of relationships never ceased to amaze Luc.

Drew gestured to the bartender for a drink, and within seconds a bottle of his favorite brew sat on the bar in front of him. "What's the score?" he asked Luc.

It took Luc a few seconds to realize Drew was referring to the game playing on the television behind the bar. He'd been so lost in thought he hadn't even noticed it was on. "No idea," he said, taking a sip of his drink.

"I'm sorry I missed the ribbon cutting at the clinic. I had a client in town looking to buy one of my mares."

"No apology necessary. If there was any way *I* could have gotten out of it, I would have."

"Is that why you look so down?"

Luc ran his thumb around the brim of his glass. "Nope."

"Anything I can do to help?"

He shook his head. "Nope."

"Maybe it would be better if I left you alone," his friend said, grabbing his beer and making a move to get up.

"No," Luc said, realizing that he was being unnecessarily rude. And frankly, he could use the company. "I'm sorry. I just got some bad news today."

"It must have been pretty bad to put you in such a foul mood."

"Julie's request to extend her visa was denied."

Drew's eyes went wide with disbelief. "No way."

"I couldn't believe it, either." Nor was he willing to accept it. But when it came to plausible ideas to stop this from happening, he was coming up short.

Drew shook his head, expression solemn. "After all she's done for this town since the storm, they should be giving her a medal, not kickin' her to the curb."

Luc's thoughts exactly.

"What are you going to do?" Drew asked.

At this point there wasn't much Luc could do. Despite her objection he'd made a call to his lawyer, who had confirmed what Julie had told him. It was a done deal. "Let her go, I guess."

"Dude, you can't do that. You can't give up on her."

"I'm out of options."

"I'll bet there's one thing you haven't considered," Drew said.

"What's that?"

"You could marry her."

Marry Julie? His best friend? Drew was right, he hadn't considered that, because it was a ridiculous notion.

"Julie is like me," he told Drew. "She's very focused on her work. Neither of us has any plans to marry."

Drew rolled his eyes, as if Luc was a moron. "It wouldn't have to be a real marriage, genius. But it would be enough to keep her in the country."

A pretend marriage? "Not only is that a preposterous idea, it's illegal. We could both get in serious trouble. We could go to prison."

Drew grinned. "Only if you get caught."

Luc could hardly believe that Drew of all people

was suggesting he break the law. "And if we do get caught, what then?"

He shrugged. "Volunteer in the prison infirmary?"

Luc glared at him and Drew laughed.

"I'm kidding. Besides, it would never come to that. No one in this town would ever question the validity of your marriage."

Confused, Luc asked, "Why is that?"

"Are you kidding? You two are inseparable. Or at least, as inseparable as two workaholics can be. Most married couples don't spend as much time together as you two do."

"We're colleagues. It's part of the job description."

"It's more than that. You just…I don't know, *fit*."

"Fit?"

"People have been waiting for you guys to hook up. And there are others who think that you must already be knocking boots."

Annoyed that anyone would make that assumption, Luc said, "People should mind their own damn business."

Drew shrugged. "Small towns."

That didn't make it any less irritating. He and Julie didn't have that kind of relationship, nor would they ever. Yeah, he may have had the hots for her when they first met, but he had been reeling from his ex-fiancée, Amelia, abruptly calling off their engagement, and Julie had just come out of an emotionally rocky relationship herself. Before they'd had a chance to get over their former significant others and explore a physical relationship together, they had become pals instead. She was his buddy, his confidante. He would never do anything to jeopardize that. "We're just friends, and that's all we'll ever be."

Looking exasperated, Drew said, "Dude, it doesn't matter. You would be married in name only. Consider the alternative."

He had, a million times since she'd hit him with the bad news. Although the term *bad news* didn't quite measure the depth of his feelings when he imagined her leaving. Living thousands of miles away. Who would he talk to? Who would remind him to pick up his dry cleaning, or share late-night Indian takeout with him in the break room on those evenings when they were both too jammed to leave the hospital?

There had been nights like that for weeks after the storm, performing surgery after surgery. Some successful, some not. While volunteering for Doctors Without Borders, he had seen his share of heartbreaking situations and managed to stay detached and objective for the most part. A disaster in his hometown was a completely different story. Without Julie to lean on, to keep him grounded, he would have been a wreck. She was his anchor, his voice of reason.

Did he love her? Absolutely. But that was very different from being *in* love. And finding a new research assistant would be a nightmare. Julie knew his work inside and out. Training someone new would take more time and energy than he cared to expend.

"I obviously don't want her to leave," Luc said. "But if we were caught and something happened to her, I would never forgive myself."

After she was gone they could keep in touch through email and social media. They could even video chat on their computers or phones, though it wouldn't be the same as having her there. But was defrauding the government and risking both her freedom and his the answer?

"I'm telling you, no one is ever going to know," Drew insisted. "Even if the truth comes out, you're a local hero. Can you name one person in town who would turn you in?"

He made a good point. And even if there was an investigation, he and Julie knew each other as well as any married couple. He had no doubt they would pass any test with flying colors. The question was: How would Julie feel about it? She was the one with the most to lose.

"I guess it couldn't hurt to bring it up and see what she thinks," he told Drew.

"Great. I suggest a small- to moderate-sized ceremony and reception at the club and a long relaxing honeymoon somewhere tropical."

A wedding was one thing, but leaving Royal? That was out of the question. "I wouldn't have time for a honeymoon. I'm needed here."

Drew laughed and slapped him on the back. "Dude, you're a brilliant and devoted physician and, yes, this town needs you, but *everyone* needs a break now and then. No one will blame you for wanting a honeymoon. When was the last time you took time off? And I mean *real* time."

Luc tried to recall, and came up blank. It had definitely been before the storm. And probably quite some time before that. A year, maybe two. Or three. He'd traveled all over the world volunteering with Doctors Without Borders. That was how he'd met Julie. Their duties had taken them to many exotic and unfamiliar destinations, but it had been no vacation. Maybe they could use a break...

Luc shook his head. He and Julie married and taking a honeymoon? Until today the thought had never even crossed his mind. And it wasn't that he didn't find her appealing, both mentally and physically. Any man would be lucky to win her heart. He'd found her so appealing when they first met, it had been a little difficult to be objective. Practicing medicine in a developing country, the accommodations weren't exactly lavish. It wasn't uncommon for all the volunteers, male and female alike, to share living quarters, where modesty took a backseat to practicality. He was used to seeing his colleagues in various stages of undress. But in the case of Julie, he would often find his gaze lingering just a little longer than most would consider appropriate. But if she'd noticed, or cared, she'd never called him out on it. The issue was exacerbated by the fact that Julie didn't have a bashful bone in her body. In his first week working with her he'd seen more skin than the first two months he'd been dating Amelia, his college sweetheart and ex-fiancée. She'd had enough body hang-ups for half a dozen women.

But he would never forget the day he'd met Julie. He had just arrived at the camp and was directed to the tent where he would sleep and store his gear. He stepped inside and there she was, sitting on her cot, wearing only panties and her bra, a sheen of sweat glistening on her golden skin, her long, reddish-brown hair pulled into a ponytail. He froze, unsure of what to do or say, thinking that his presence there would offend her. But Julie hadn't batted an eyelash.

"You must be Lucas," she said, unfazed, rising from

her cot to shake his hand while he stood there, caught somewhere between embarrassment and arousal. It was the first of many times he'd seen her without her clothes on, but that particular memory stood out in his mind.

He and Julie had seen each other at their best, inventing surgical tools and techniques that they knew would change the face of modern surgery, and at their worst, unwashed and unshaven for weeks on end covered in bug bites from every critter imaginable. They had been to hell and back together, and they always, under any circumstance, had each other's back. Was this situation any different? Didn't he owe it to her?

It was becoming less of a question of why, and more of a question of why not. "You really think this could work?" he asked Drew, feeling a glimmer of hope.

"You would have to make it convincing," Drew said.

"Convincing how?"

"Well, she would have to move in with you."

Of course as a married couple they would have to live together. He and his mother had more than enough space, and four spare bedrooms for her to choose from. "What else?"

"In public you would have to look as if you're in love. You know, hold hands, kiss…stuff like that."

There was a time when he'd wondered what it would be like to kiss Julie. A real kiss, not her usual peck on the cheek when she hugged him goodbye. How would her lips feel pressed against his? How would she taste?

The tug of lust in his boxers caught him completely off guard. What the hell was wrong with him?

He cleared his throat and took a deep swallow of Scotch. "I could do that."

"No one else can know it's not real. We keep it

right here, between us," Drew said. "You know you can trust me."

Trusting Drew wasn't the issue. He knew that any one of his club brothers would lay down their life for him. The whole idea hinged on Julie's willingness to break the law and play house with him for heaven only knew how long. And her willingness to play the part convincingly.

It was something he would have to investigate thoroughly on his own before bringing it up to her. Talk to his attorney about the legalities. Make a list of the pros and cons.

"I'll talk to her," he told Drew.

"Who knows," Drew said with a sly grin, "you two might actually fall in love."

That's where Drew was wrong. If Luc and Julie were meant to fall in love, meant to be a couple, it would have happened a long time ago.

Julie sat in her office the next day, eyes darting nervously from the work on her desk to the clock on the wall. She was due to meet Luc in the atrium for a late lunch in fifteen minutes. Seeing her best friend had never been cause for a case of the jitters, but this was different: this had her heart thumping, her hands trembling and her stomach tied in knots. She was planning to ask Luc a favor, the biggest and most important favor she had ever asked him. Ever asked *anyone*. But if there was a single person on the planet she could count on to come through for her, it was Luc. More so than her own sister, who could be flighty at best. It sometimes took her days or even a week to answer a text or email. Sometimes she didn't answer at all.

Luc was truly the only person in her life who she could count on unconditionally. And if everything went as she hoped, she would be able to stay in the country indefinitely. Worst case, Luc would laugh in her face, and she would be on her way back to her native home, where she had only distant family left and no friends to speak of.

In the event that Luc said no, she would spend the rest of her time in the US tying up loose ends regarding the research on Luc's latest invention. She had reports to file and interviews to transcribe so that the switch to his new assistant would be a smooth one. Though the idea of someone else finishing her work left an empty feeling in the pit of her stomach.

The sudden rap on her office door startled her out of her musings. She looked up and was surprised to see Luc standing there. She checked the clock. She still had ten minutes to spare.

"Can I come in?" he asked. He wore scrubs under his lab coat, meaning he must have had a surgery scheduled that morning.

"Of course," she said, gesturing him in. "I thought we were meeting in the atrium. Did I get the time wrong?"

"Nope." He stepped into her office, which wasn't much larger than a small walk-in closet, and as he did, she felt as if all the breathable air disappeared from the room. It would explain the dizzy feeling in her head, the frantic beat of her heart.

What was wrong with her? She'd never been nervous around Luc. The truth is, she never got nervous about much of anything. Especially Luc. Everything about him, from his slow, easy grin and low, patient voice to his dark, compassionate eyes, naturally put people at ease. He could be intimidating as hell when he wanted to be. She'd seen it. But unless the situation warranted it, he chose not to be.

"I wanted a minute to talk in private," he said, snapping the door closed behind him. He crossed the two steps to her desk and sat on the edge. She could be mistaken, but he looked a little uneasy, which wasn't like him at all.

"There's something I need to ask you," he said.

What a coincidence. "There's something I need to ask you, too."

"Why don't I go first," he said.

Now that she'd worked up the nerve, she couldn't back down. "I think I should go first."

"What I have to say might impact what you have to say."

All the more reason to say it right now. The last thing she wanted was to make a huge deal about this. If she made a fool of herself, so be it.

It sure wouldn't be the first time.

Three

Luc was watching her expectantly, and she knew that the longer she dragged this out, the harder it would be. What she was about to ask him was no small favor. She wouldn't blame him at all if he said no.

Okay, Jules, you can do this.

Hoping he didn't hear the slight quiver in her voice, notice her unsteady hands or the erratic flutter of her pulse, she said, "I may have come up with a way to stay in the country. But I need your help."

His brow rose expectantly. "What kind of help?"

Her heart lodged in her throat, so when she opened her mouth to speak, nothing came out. For several seconds she sat there like a fool, the words frozen in her vocal cords.

Wearing a quirky smile, Luc asked, "Are you okay?"

Yes and no.

She was being silly. He was her best friend. Even if he said no, it wouldn't change anything. Hopefully it would only be slightly humiliating.

Come on, Jules, just say it.

Gathering her courage, she said, "You know that I really don't want to leave the US."

"And I don't want you to leave," he said.

"Royal has become my home. I feel like I belong here."

"You do belong here." He said it as if there were no question in his mind. "And you know that I'll do anything I can to help. As a matter of fact—"

"Please, let me finish." Earnest as he appeared, he might want to take that back when she told him her plan. "I've looked into every possible avenue, but there's only one way I've come up with that will assure I can stay."

She paused taking a deep, empowering breath. Then another.

"Are you going to tell me," he asked, looking mildly amused. "Or do you want me to guess?"

Oh, for Pete's sake, just say it, Jules. "We could get married. Temporarily of course," she added swiftly. "Just until I can earn my citizenship. Then we can get a quickie divorce and pretend it never happened. I'll sign a contract or a prenup. Whatever makes you most comfortable."

Luc blinked, then blinked again, and then he burst out laughing.

Wow. There it was. Her worst nightmare realized.

"You're right," she said, quickly backtracking. "It was a ridiculous idea. I don't know what I was thinking." She shot to her feet, when what she really wanted to do was curl up in the fetal position and wallow in shame. "Let's forget I said anything and go have lunch."

She tried to duck past him, and he wrapped a very large but gentle hand around the upper part of her left arm.

"Just hold on a minute," he said in that firm but patient way of his. From anyone else it would have come off as condescending. "It is *not* ridiculous. Not at all. I'm laughing because I came here to suggest the exact same thing."

It was her turn to blink in surprise. Did he mean that, or was he just trying to make her feel less stupid. "Seriously?"

"But it is a legally and morally gray area. I wasn't sure if you would be willing to risk breaking the law."

Desperate times required desperate measures. "I'm willing if you are."

"We can't risk anyone else knowing the truth."

"I won't tell if you don't."

"Drew knows. He's the one who suggested it. But we can trust him. And I won't lie to my mother."

Julie had never known Drew to be anything but a stand-up guy. If Luc trusted him, so would she. And she would never expect Luc to lie to Elizabeth, nor would she want him to.

Julie had no one else to tell, except her sister, Jennifer, who probably wouldn't care anyway. When she married her husband, an older, wealthy man she'd met on a trip to New York, he became the center of her life. She quit college and set her sights on being the perfect trophy wife. Between charity balls and country club brunches with the other trophy wives in her elite social circle, she had little time for her nomadic, unsophisticated sister.

Though she had never actually met Jennifer's husband—nor did she care to—her sister's description of him gave Julie a bad feeling. He sounded very controlling, like their father. But now was not the time to dredge up those old memories. She had promised herself a long time ago that she would never look back in regret, but instead learn from her past and always move forward. Always strive to better herself. Marrying Luc, though completely unexpected, would be just another leg of her journey.

"Having second thoughts already?" Luc asked, and she realized she was frowning.

"No, of course not. Just wondering what happens next."

"Drew suggested we have the ceremony and reception at the club and we have to do it soon."

"How soon?"

"How's this Saturday afternoon looking for you?"

This Saturday? That was only five days away. She knew absolutely zero about planning a wedding, but less than a week sounded ridiculously fast. "Is it even possible to put a wedding together that quickly? And what about immigration? Don't we have to have an interview or something?"

"My attorney is taking care of all of that. And as for the wedding, we'll keep it simple. Close friends only. Very informal."

"I don't even know where to start."

"All you need to do is find a dress. And a maid of honor. I'll take care of the rest."

Of all her friends in Royal, Lark Taylor was the closest. They'd met during the first few weeks of the cleanup efforts and became fast friends. She was a nurse in the intensive care unit at the hospital. They often took coffee breaks together, and sometimes went out for drinks after work. She was planning her own wedding to Keaton Holt, a longtime Cattleman's Club member, so perhaps she could give Julie a few pointers.

"We'll have to kiss," she heard Luc say, and it took her brain a second to catch up with her ears.

"Kiss?"

"During the ceremony," he said.

"Oh…right." She hadn't considered that. She thought about kissing Luc and a peculiar little shiver cascaded down the length of her spine. Back when she first met him, she used to think about the two of them doing a lot more than just kissing, but he had been too hung up on Amelia and their recently broken engagement to even think about another woman. So hung up that he left his life in Royal behind and traveled halfway around the world with Doctors Without Borders.

A recent dumpee herself, she'd been just as confused and vulnerable at the time, and she knew there was nothing worse for the ego than a rebound relationship. They were, and always would be, better off as friends. In her experience, it was usually one or the other. Mixing sex and friendship would only end in disaster.

"Is that a problem?" Luc asked.

She blinked. "Problem?"

"Us kissing. You got an odd look on your face."

Had she? "It's no problem at all," she assured him, but if that was true, why did her stomach bottom out when she imagined his lips on hers. It had been a long time since she'd been kissed by anyone. Maybe too long.

"We'll have to start acting like a married couple," he said.

"In what way?"

"You'll have to move in with me."

She hadn't really considered that, but of course a married couple would live together. Having separate residences would raise a very bright red flag. Since Julie left home, when she wasn't volunteering abroad, she'd lived alone. She liked the freedom of answering to no one but herself, of doing what she wanted to do, when she wanted to do it. That would be hard to give up.

As if Luc read her mind, he added, "Nothing in our relationship is going to change. We only have to make it look as if it has."

But by pretending that it changed, by making it look that way to everyone else, wasn't that in itself a change? *Ugh.* She never realized how complicated this could be. She could already feel the walls closing in on her.

"Look," he said, and this time he was the one frowning. "If any of this makes you uncomfortable, we don't have to do it. I want you to stay in the US, and I'll do whatever I can to help make that happen, but if it's going to cause a rift in our friendship, maybe it's not worth it."

"I'm just used to living on my own. The idea of changing that is a little intimidating. But it is worth it. And I don't want you to think that I'm not grateful. I am."

"I know you are." He smiled and laid a hand on her forearm, and the feel of his skin against hers gave her that little shiver again. What the heck was going on? She never used to shiver like that when he touched her. She was sure it was due only to the stress of her situation.

What else could it possibly be?

"It's bad, isn't it?" Julie looked up at Lark, her maid of honor, in the dressing room mirror at the Cattleman's

Club. Julie was on her third attempt of giving herself "smoky eyes." But she looked more like a cheap street walker than a bride.

"When it comes to eyeliner and shadow, especially for someone as naturally pretty as you, I think less is more," Lark said, which was her kind way of telling Julie to give it up.

"Oh my God, what a mess," Julie said, swiping at her eyes with a damp cloth. It had looked pretty simple in the instructional video she'd found online, but her technique lacked a certain…finesse. Which is why she never wore the stuff.

Her father had lived by very traditional values and as teens, Julie and her sister had been forbidden to use makeup of any kind. Or wear pants. Dresses and skirts were the only acceptable attire for a female in her father's home, and Julie had played the role of obedient daughter very well. It was easier not to make waves. She concentrated on her studies and getting into a good college. She never did develop the desire to wear makeup, but after eighteen years of wearing only skirts and dresses, she swore she would never wear anything but pants. Yet here she was now in a newly purchased, off-white, silk shift dress, which she had to admit hung nicely on her athletic frame. But with her raccoon eyes Luc was going to take one look at her and run in the opposite direction.

Her sister, the queen of all things girly and impractical, would have been a big help right about now but she wasn't answering calls or texts. If it was anyone but Jennifer, Julie might have worried, but that was typical for her sister. She was either completely distant and unreliable, or smothering Julie with her sisterly love. There was no middle ground.

"I suck at this," she said.

"Maybe just a little mascara and liner," Lark suggested, with a sympathetic smile. "Would you like me to help?"

Julie looked up at her with pleading, raccoon eyes. "Yes, please."

Lark worked her magic and she was right. Julie was lucky to have been blessed with smooth, clear skin, and just a touch of liner and mascara and a little clear gloss on her lips subtly enhanced her features.

"You're a genius," she told Lark.

"And you look beautiful," Lark said, smiling and stepping back to admire her work. "Lucas is a lucky man. And forgive me for saying, but it's about darned time you two tied the knot."

Julie had heard that same remark from a dozen people since she and Luc made the announcement earlier that week. "It doesn't seem…*sudden*?"

"I always suspected you and Luc had something going—I think everyone has—but you're a very private person, so I didn't want to ask. I figured that if you wanted me to know, or needed to talk about it, you would tell me."

If there had been anything to tell, Julie probably would have.

There was a rap on the dressing room door and Lark's sister Skye stepped into the dressing room. She looked surprisingly healthy for someone still recovering from a near-fatal car crash during the tornado. Luc had performed an emergency cesarean to save her unborn child, and her injuries had been so severe she'd been in a coma for four months. Until Skye was well enough to care for her daughter, Lark had taken responsibility for Baby Grace, who was the sweetest most adorable infant Julie had ever seen.

"It's time," Skye said, then sighed wistfully. "You look beautiful. Luc is a lucky guy."

Julie took a good look at herself in the mirror, spinning in a circle to get every angle. Not half-bad.

Though she usually kept her hair pulled up into a ponytail, she'd worn it down today, in loose, soft curls that tumbled across her shoulders. She'd even put on her mother's diamond earrings. It was the only thing of her mother's that she had left. In his grief after she died, Julie's father had removed every trace of his wife from their home. Photos, personal items, anything that reminded him of her. Julie had only been four at the time, but she remembered sitting on her parents' bed, crying as she watched their housekeeper clear out her mother's closet, shoving her clothes into black trash bags.

Between his wife's death and having a newborn infant to care for, her father seemed to forget that he had another child who was mixed up and lonely and desperate for the unconditional love and affection her mother had always given so freely. Within weeks of her death he'd hired a nanny and began traveling extensively. He had never been what anyone would consider an attentive father, but after her mother's death he had become virtually nonexistent.

Julie breathed deep to ease the knot of sadness in her chest, the burn of tears behind her eyes. Now was not the time to think about her less than ideal childhood. God forbid she start crying and ruin her makeup.

"How are you doing?" Lark asked. "You nervous?"

Julie shook her head. This wasn't going to be a real marriage, so what reason did she have to be nervous?

Though they wouldn't be married for long, she had insisted on a prenup. To protect not just his interests, but her own, as well. She'd never been the type to flaunt her wealth, but with the inheritance her father had left her and her sister, and a little savvy investing, Julie was pretty much set for life. A simple, no frills life, but that was fine with her. She didn't need much.

"So, are you ready?" Lark asked, and Julie turned to find her and Skye watching her expectantly.

After one more quick glance in the mirror, she nodded and told her friends, "Let's do this."

Four

With so little time to plan the wedding, Drew had volunteered to put a guest list together for Luc. But now, as Luc stood with Drew at his side, waiting for the ceremony to begin, scanning row upon row of guests idly chatting, he was beginning to think that had been a bad idea. It seemed as if half the town was there.

He leaned in close to Drew and said in a harsh whisper, "This is your idea of small and intimate?"

"Just helping to make it convincing," Drew said with a wry smile. It was obvious to Luc that he was thoroughly enjoying himself. "Are you nervous?"

"Of course not." What reason did he have to be? This was nothing more than a business arrangement between friends. In fact, he felt exceedingly calm. A little bored even.

"All grooms get nervous," Drew persisted.

"But I'm not a real groom, am I?"

"Look around you. This sure looks real to me. Besides, you can't argue with a marriage license."

Okay, so maybe he was a real groom, but not in the traditional sense. They would be married, but not really married. Together, but not really together.

Luc glanced over at his mother, who sat in her

wheelchair in the front row, an encouraging smile on her face. When he told her about the marriage she was beside herself excited, even when he explained the true nature of the situation.

"It's just a way to keep Julie in the States," he'd explained.

"Of course it is," she'd said with a twinkle in her eyes, as if she knew something he didn't. If she believed it to be anything more than a friend helping out another friend, if she had her heart set on Luc and Julie falling in love, she would be sorely disappointed.

Stella Daniels, who was officiating, touched Luc's shoulder and said softly, "Words cannot express how happy I am for the two of you. And forgive me for saying this, but it's about damned time."

He kept a smile planted firmly on his lips, but he felt a distinct twinge of guilt. He'd heard many similar remarks this past week, and as much as he hated the idea of lying to everyone, he and Julie had no choice.

The music started and everyone turned to the doorway where Lark stood, carrying a small bouquet of miniature yellow roses—Julie's favorite color.

Here we go, Luc thought, his stomach bottoming out.

Okay, so, maybe he was a *little* nervous.

Lark made her trip down the aisle, but Luc's attention remained fixed on the doorway, anticipation tying his stomach into knots. Then the "Wedding March" started and Julie appeared in the doorway, and all Luc could think was *wow*.

Rarely did he see Julie with her hair down, and in all the time he'd known her he couldn't recall ever seeing her in a dress. Cut several inches above the knee, it was just long enough to be tasteful, but short enough to showcase her toned, suntanned calves and a little bit of thigh...

Whoa, he thought, as his pulse picked up speed. This was Julie he was gawking at, his best friend. But damn, who could blame him? She looked stunning and sexy and as his eyes met and locked on hers, he experienced a distinct tug of sexual attraction. Bordering on red-hot lust.

Talk about getting caught up in the moment. If this kept up he was going to need a serious attitude adjustment.

Everyone stood and she started down the aisle, walking alone, holding a single long-stemmed yellow rose, looking cool and composed, as if she did this sort of thing all the time. This may have been a "pretend" wedding, but in that moment it couldn't have felt more real to him, and despite her cool exterior, when Julie faced him and he took her hands, they were trembling.

Stella began the ceremony, but he was so focused on Julie, the mayor's words all seemed to run together. It was almost as if he was really seeing Julie for the first time. And though he'd been to more weddings than he could count, as they recited their vows, he realized he'd never really grasped the gravity of the words. Real marriage or not, as he slid the platinum band on her ring finger—she'd balked at the idea of a diamond— he pledged to himself that as long as they were married, he would honor those vows.

Then came the part he'd been most anticipating. The kiss to seal the deal. They had to make it look convincing. Too chaste or formal and it might make people suspicious; too passionate and Julie might crack him one. Probably not here at the wedding, but later, when they were alone.

There was another possibility. One he hadn't truly considered until just now. What if he kissed her, and he liked it? So much so that he wanted to do it again. And even more intriguing was the possibility that she might like it, too.

"You may kiss the bride," Stella said, and Julie's pulse jumped as Luc, seemingly in ultra slow motion, bent his head. The entire ceremony had been a bit surreal, as if she were standing outside of her body watching herself. But this? This was very real.

Her chin lifted in anticipation, and she began to wonder if this was something they should have rehearsed ahead of time. No one's first kiss should have an audience, yet here they stood with dozens of pairs of eyes planted firmly on them.

Oh boy, what had they gotten themselves into?

Luc reached up, his hand gently cupping her cheek, and her knees went weak. His lips brushed softly across hers, seeming to linger undecidedly between obligation and curiosity, and a sound, like a soft moan, slipped unexpectedly from her lips. Without realizing she'd even moved, her hands were on his chest and curling into the lapels of his suit jacket, pulling him closer. If it hadn't been for the sudden round of applause, and the hoots and howls from their guests, she would have gone right on kissing him. As their lips parted and she looked up into his eyes, she could see that he was equally perplexed. And as lame and juvenile as it sounded, she heard herself saying softly, "Wow, you're really good at that."

A wry grin tipped up the corners of his lips. "So are you."

Her kissing skills, and his, were irrelevant. So why the shiver of pleasure? The weak-kneed feeling of anticipation? There was nothing to anticipate. They were married and she was a legal resident. As devious plans go, this one was playing out exactly as they'd expected. The hard part was over.

With all the handshaking and hugs, the walk back down the aisle took so long that when they finally made it to the room where the reception was being held, people were already sipping very expensive champagne and nibbling on the appetizers catered by a restaurant in town that had reopened its doors just last week. Though she distinctly remembered Luc saying it would be small and intimate, it looked to Julie as if nearly every member of the Cattleman's Club and their significant others were in attendance.

She looked up at Luc. "Small and intimate, huh?"

"I put Drew in charge of the guest list," he said, nabbing two glasses of champagne from a passing waiter and handing one to her. "So if you have a bone to pick, it's with him. And forgive me for saying it, but you look positively stunning."

Forgive him? His words made her feel dizzy with pleasure. "If it wasn't for Lark's help, you would have married a raccoon."

He regarded her with a curious expression.

She laughed and shook her head. "Never mind."

Somewhere behind her Julie heard the sharp tink of metal on glass and turned to see Skye tapping her champagne flute with the tines of her fork. Her husband, Jake, mirrored her actions, then several other guests joined in, all turning to look at Julie and Luc as if they were waiting for them to do or say something.

She heard Luc mumble something under his breath, and asked him in a hushed voice, "What are they doing?"

"They want us to kiss."

Julie blinked. "Kiss?"

Luc shrugged. "It's tradition."

And he couldn't have warned her about this? So she could at least prepare herself. "I've never been to an American wedding. You're saying we have to kiss? Right now? In front of all these people?"

"If we want them to stop."

Considering the rising decibel level, if she and Luc didn't kiss, someone was bound to shatter something. Besides, it had been so nice kissing him the first time. One more time wouldn't hurt, right? Who was she to question the tradition.

"Well, if we have to," she said.

Luc bent his head and brushed a very brief and chaste kiss across her lips, but the tinking didn't stop.

"You can do better than that," someone shouted.

Her heart did a back-and-forth shimmy in her chest. Oh boy, this could wind up being a very long evening.

Luc gazed at her questioningly, his eyes saying it would be best if they appeased the crowd. Julie shrugged, whispering, "We have to make it look real, I guess."

She tried to play it cool, but on the inside she was trembling as Luc cupped the back of her head, his hand sliding through her hair, fingers tangling in the curls. And if that didn't feel nice enough, his kiss nearly did her in. When his tongue swept across her lower lip she felt it like an electrical charge, as if every cell in her body came alive all at once. But then it was over and she had to fight the urge to toss her champagne glass aside, grab the lapels of his jacket and pull him in for more.

It must have been sufficient for the guests, because the tinking faded out, only to start up again a few minutes later, instigated this time by Paige Richardson, who stood beside her brother-in-law Colby.

Colby was Aaron Nichols's partner in R&N Builders, which was almost single-handedly responsible for rebuilding the town after the tornado. And though Julie knew him to be a friendly and outgoing, all-around nice guy, the deep furrow in Colby's brow said something was troubling him.

The tinking rose to an unreasonable level and Julie could swear that every single guest had joined in.

She looked up at Luc, who appeared as amused as he was apologetic. "I have the feeling we're going to be doing a lot of kissing today."

"So do I." And what a hardship that would be. *Not.* And even if he was the worst kisser on the planet, her citizenship depended on it. It was her obligation to make this marriage look as real as possible. Because if she were to be discovered, and someone proved the marriage was a sham, she would go down hard and take Luc with her. That was not an option.

Before he could make a move, to change things up a bit, she set her empty champagne flute down, slid her arms around his neck and kissed him first. A no-holds-barred, knock-him-on-his-butt kiss that jump-started her pulse and made her tingle in places she didn't even know she could tingle. His arms went around her and he tugged her against him. He cupped her behind and rocked his pelvis against her stomach. She gasped against his lips when she felt the thick ridge behind his zipper. Obviously he was just as into this as she was, and not at all shy about letting her know it. If not for his suit jacket, everyone else would probably know, too.

This time when they parted he was wearing a wry, sexy smile, and whispered, without a trace of contrition, "What can I say. I'm a guy."

This was a side of him she'd never seen before. Playfully sexy and a little risqué. She wanted nothing more than to be alone with him, and at the same time felt thankful for their guests. Until they both had time to settle down, being alone together might be a bad idea.

No, not *might*, it *would* be.

As the evening progressed, each subsequent kiss was more brazen and more ardent than the last, his touch as bold as it was scandalous.

It went on like that for a good hour before, to Julie's disappointment, the kiss requests finally began to taper off until they stopped altogether. People began to leave, until only their core group of friends remained.

Though Julie had already had far too much champagne, she headed to the bar for another drink and Beth followed her. "This has been so much fun," she told Julie.

"I think so, too."

"Your sister couldn't make it?"

Julie had texted her, called her and sent her a detailed email about the situation, but still no reply. Her husband traveled extensively for business and Jennifer often accompanied him, occasionally for weeks at a time. "I couldn't get ahold of her. They're probably out of the country."

"That's too bad."

Julie shrugged. "It was awfully last-minute."

"It certainly was. Which brings me to my next question. What was it like making out with your best friend?"

Julie just stood there, mouth agape. Did she mean—?

"Drew told me. We don't keep secrets from each other."

Now Drew, Beth, Luc's mother and her sister all knew the truth?

"Don't worry, I won't tell a soul," Beth assured her. "And for what it's worth, you gave a very convincing performance."

And Julie had relished every moment. Much more than she meant to, or should have. "He's a good kisser."

Beth grinned. "So I gathered. I'll bet he's good at a lot of things."

Her suggestive grin left no question as to what she was implying. And Julie knew she was probably right. She was dying to know how it would feel, their bodies intertwined, his weight pushing her into the mattress...

A ripple of heat coursed through her veins and she could feel her cheeks growing hot. Definitely not something she should be thinking about. "I'm sure he is," she told Beth. "But I'll never find out."

"The way Luc looks at you, I get the feeling you won't have a choice."

No choice? "What is it you think he'll do? Tie me down and make passionate love to me?"

Beth's smile widened. "One can hope."

Oh God, she was right. If Luc wanted Julie in his bed, restraining her wouldn't be necessary.

Ugh, *no*. She was not going to sleep with him. The combination of champagne and all that kissing was screwing with her brain, flooding it with hormones, or pheromones, or some other kind of mones. They were friends and that's all they would ever be.

"Where are you two going for your honeymoon?" Beth asked.

"Nowhere. Luc has a new patient to evaluate this week. A little boy who needs spinal surgery. Besides, you know how he is about leaving the hospital for any extended amount of time. Or his mother. She's still weak from her last hospital stay."

"Most new brides would expect to be put first."

Julie shrugged. "I guess I'm not like most new brides. I can't expect him to rearrange his whole life just because we're married. I wouldn't want him to."

Luc's ex-fiancée had been one of those women. Like any young resident, Luc had been required to work insane hours. It was part of the job. Amelia demanded more attention than he was able to give, which was what ultimately caused their split. The way Luc described her, she was spoiled and snotty, always wanting things her way. Even if she had married him, Julie doubted it would have lasted.

"A lot of women go into a marriage thinking they can change their spouse," Beth said.

"That's ridiculous. If you don't love the person for who they are, why marry them in the first place?"

Beth grinned. "Luc is a lucky man."

Julie wasn't sure what she meant by that, and she didn't ask. Drinks in hand, they rejoined the others.

Luc, Colby and Whit Daltry, owner of Daltry Property Management, were discussing the hospital, and how much money it would take to rebuild the damaged portion. Stella and her husband, Aaron, were discussing baby formula options with Lark and Skye, who both had plenty of information on all things baby. Paige, who Julie noticed had been avoiding her brother-in-law like the plague all evening and pretending not to see the looks he kept shooting her way, sat silently.

Beth took her seat at the table where they had all congregated, and for a minute Julie stood there watching everyone, soaking it all in, a feeling of peace and happiness warming her heart. The town, the people… they were so familiar to her now and so accepting. This was, without question, home.

"Come sit down," Luc said, holding out his hand for her to take. She twined her fingers through his, intending to sit in the empty chair beside him, but Luc had other ideas. He tugged her down onto his lap instead, and up went her heart, right into her throat. He slipped one arm around her and settled his palm against her stomach, his thumb grazing the underside of her breast as he did, and the other hand came to rest on her bare knee. What if that hand were to slide up the inside of her thigh under her dress? Would she stop him? *Could* she?

She glanced over at Beth, whose smile seemed to say, *I told you so.*

She realized just then, with no small amount of anticipation, that if Luc decided he wanted her, there wasn't a damned thing she could do about it.

Five

They didn't get home until eleven—it was a little weird to think of Luc's house as home—and they were both bushed. It had been a long and exhausting evening spent in a near-constant state of arousal, but now it was time to shut it down. The wedding was over and they were back to being friends.

Luc walked her to her bedroom door, which was directly across the hall from his own. She expected a hug and a kiss, even if it was just on her cheek, but she got neither.

"Well, good night," he said, shutting the door to his room firmly behind him.

She stood in the hallway alone, wondering what just happened. After having his hands on her all evening, that was the best he could do? He could just walk away without even acknowledging it?

What if he was having second thoughts? What if he realized he didn't want to be married? He'd been exceedingly quiet on the drive home—there was that word again...*home*. He could be in his room right now, pacing the floor in a panic, thinking that maybe they should get the marriage annulled.

There was no way she could fall asleep with this

hanging over her. She had to know what was going on in his head, before she let herself get too comfortable.

Was she really home, or wasn't she?

Taking a minute or two to think it over, she devised a genius plan to engage him in a conversation. Once she got him talking, she could spring her suspicions on him and see how he reacted.

Feeling confident that she was doing the right thing, she rapped softly on his door. He opened it several seconds later wearing silk pajama bottoms slung low on his hips, his chest bare.

Oh good Lord.

She had seen him bare chested plenty of times in the past, but it occurred to her that she had never actually *seen* him. Only now did she really notice and appreciate the lean muscles of his torso. The sprinkling of dark hair that circled his navel and disappeared under his waistband. Wide chest, above average pecs. He was beautiful.

He hadn't even touched her and she was feeling all tingly again.

He leaned against the doorjamb. "Everything okay?"

"I'm sorry to bother you, but I wondered if you could unzip me. My dress, I mean."

His brow rose. "Seriously?"

Was that such an odd request? "Yes, seriously. I can't reach it."

He folded his arms, looking amused. And sexy as hell. How had she not noticed before how insanely gorgeous he was? Had she been wearing blinders all these years?

"So what you're telling me is that if I weren't here

to unzip you, you would be stuck in your dress in-definitely?"

She blinked. "Well…no, but—"

"If you're going to make up an excuse to come to my room, you could be a little more imaginative, don't you think?"

Boy, did he have her number.

"You were so quiet on the way home I was afraid something was wrong," she said. "I thought that maybe you were having second thoughts about this."

"Then, why didn't you just say that?"

Because…well, she didn't exactly know why. She'd never had a problem being totally honest with him before they were married. Maybe this time she was afraid of the answer she might get. But she had to know.

"So, are you?" she asked him.

"Am I what?"

"Having second thoughts?"

He shook his head and said, "Nope."

She waited for more, for some sort of assurance everything was fine, but he just stood there looking at her.

Oooookay.

"You were very distant on the ride home. Then we got here and, well…" Why was this so hard to say? He wasn't helping matters, standing there all sexy and gorgeous, his eyes locked on hers.

"We got here and what?"

"We're married now. I figured you would at least hug me good night or something. Maybe a kiss on the cheek?"

"You don't want me to do that."

"I don't?"

"Nope."

"Why not?"

"Suffice it to say, I'm a little...overstimulated."

Oh, this was interesting. Now they were getting somewhere. "So, you're turned on."

He trained his eyes on her and...*whoa*. The heat smoldering in their dark depths could have burned a hole through her dress. That was a definite yes. Her heart flip-flopped, making her pulse race and her mouth go dry.

"You want the truth?" he said.

She nodded.

He leaned in just a little closer. "I wanted everyone to leave the reception so I could lock the door, strip you naked, spread you on the table and lick wedding cake off every inch of your body."

"*Every* inch?"

He grinned. "*Every* inch."

She knew there was a reason she should have wrapped up the leftover cake and brought it home.

"However," he added, "friends don't do that."

"Some friends do. And I'm pretty sure I read somewhere that we have to consummate the marriage to make it official and legally binding."

"And I'm pretty sure you just made that up."

Yes, she had made it up. But she needed to kiss him again, feel his hands on her. Right now. Without her clothes getting in the way. It was their wedding night for heaven's sake. Hadn't she earned the right to jump his bones? Just this once? Would that really be such a terrible thing? Their friendship was solid. It would take a lot more than one night of sex to come between them. Or even two or three nights.

His pajama bottoms did little to hide the erection

pushing outward as if it was reaching for her touch. And oh, did she want to touch him.

One strategically placed hand and he would be toast. Not to toot her own horn, but she knew her way around the male body. He wouldn't be able to resist her, and he damn sure would walk away thoroughly satisfied. "So, you don't think we should sleep together?"

"I didn't say that."

What did he want her to do? Get down on her knees and beg? "You didn't *not* say it, either."

"It's been an emotional day, and we've had a lot to drink—"

"Oh, I get it. Say no more. I would never want you to, you know, embarrass yourself."

His brows jumped upward. He knew she was up to something, and clearly he was enjoying the game just as much as she was. Verbal foreplay was highly underrated.

"Embarrass myself how?"

"You're worried about your performance. Alcohol can make things a little, well, limp."

He glanced down to his crotch, then back up to her. "That's obviously not the case."

No, it wasn't. *And enough playing around already.* She was ready to get to the good stuff.

"Are you sure?" She reached out and wrapped her hand around his hard-on through his pajamas, giving it a firm squeeze. Holy cow, he was *big.*

Luc groaned and leaned into her hand, clutching the doorjamb in a white-knuckled grip, his eyes never leaving her face. He was hers, no question.

"I guess you're right—everything seems to be in working order. But just to be sure…" She slipped her hand under his waistband and around his erection, skin against skin, giving it a couple of slow strokes, teasing the tip with the pad of her thumb. "Feels good to me."

His eyes turned black with desire. She almost had him. Most men would have caved by now, but Luc had a steel will.

"You're positively sure you want to do this?" he said.

At this point, how could he even ask her that? Wasn't it obvious that she wanted him? "Without a doubt."

"You're not worried that it will change things between us?"

"One time? It's not as if we're going to make a habit of this." She squeezed and felt him pulse against her palm. "Besides, we spent half the day making out and now I'm standing here with my hand in your pants. If something was going to change, wouldn't it have already?"

"So what you're saying is, the damage is already done?"

"In a manner of speaking." He was making a bigger deal out of this than was warranted. But he was a planner. He liked to think ahead, plot out his every move. Which, she supposed, was why he was such an accomplished surgeon. She, on the other hand, was more of a live-in-the-moment, fly-by-the-seat-of-her-pants girl. They sat on opposite ends of the spectrum. He was all about duty and honor and doing the right thing. She believed in trying new things and taking chances. Living life to the fullest and going where the wind took her.

Tonight, the wind was blowing her in the direction of his bed.

Knowing Luc the way she did, she knew exactly

how this would play out. He would caress her as he slowly removed her clothes, taking his time. Her pleasure would be his main priority because that's the kind of man he was. Always putting the needs of others before his own. She would let him take his time, and when they were both good and worked up, she would take over. If this was going to be the only time they slept together, she planned to give him a night that he would never forget. And if they decided to do it again, well, that was okay, too.

That was her plan at least, but Luc was playing by a totally different set of rules. He looked at her as if he were a hunter stalking its prey, and then he lunged and went all caveman on her. One second her feet were on the ground, and the next, she was hanging over his shoulder, which was more than wide enough to accommodate her. She gasped and clutched his back, dizzy with desire and a little disoriented as he kicked the door closed and carried her across the room to his bed. And there was nothing gentle about the way he tossed her down on the comforter.

Who was this man and why was she just now meeting him? And how, after all these years of friendship, could she have pegged him so wrong?

He knelt on the mattress beside her, his hand resting on her inner thigh, and all she could think was *more*. He slid the hand up under the hem of her dress. His fingertips grazed the crotch of her panties, no more than a tickle. She sucked in a breath and her thighs parted, straining against the skirt of her dress.

He pulled his hand away and her back arched, her body seeking out his touch. "Did I mention how sexy you look in this dress?"

"Thanks. I don't usually wear them," she said, the words coming out all breathy and uneven. She couldn't seem to pull enough air into her lungs. What happened to all the oxygen?

"I'm going to buy you a dozen more."

If this was the reaction she got when she wore a dress, maybe that would be a bad idea. Or a good one. She wasn't sure. Suddenly everything felt backward and upside down.

He was back under her dress, tugging her panties down. There was nothing slow about the way he undressed her. Or gentle. Then he took his pajama bottoms off...

Yikes. He wouldn't be the only one walking away satisfied. This was going to be fun.

She tried to push him onto his back but it was like trying to move a brick wall. She wound up on her back instead, and when she reached out to touch him, he pinned her arms over her head, a move that would normally trigger a sense of panic. He wouldn't let her take control, which both frustrated and aroused her. But she knew deep in her heart that she was safe with him. She usually felt threatened by sexually aggressive men, but she *wanted* him to dominate her. She trusted Luc, so she did something she had never done before. She dropped her guard and let go, let him be the one in charge.

It was as cathartic as it was exciting. And Luc held nothing back, stroking here, kissing there. Licking and biting and flipping her around until she felt like a pretzel, so he could explore every inch of her body. He knew exactly what she liked, what she needed, without her having to say a thing. Besides, she was too busy gasping and moaning to form intelligible words. He teased her relentlessly. And every time she thought she was getting the upper hand, he turned the tables on her again. She'd orgasmed twice, and was headlong into number three when he rolled her onto her back and settled over her.

He didn't ask her if she was ready, or if she was having second thoughts. They were both too far gone for that. He parted her thighs with his knee and thrust inside her. She savored the sweet stretch of her body accepting him, his weight pressing her into the mattress as he eased back, then thrust again. And again, picking up speed, but with more hip action this time. Pretty much all she could do was wrap her legs around his hips and hang on for the ride. Pleasure rippled through her in hot waves, her body clenching down around him like a vise as orgasm number three took hold.

After that things got very fuzzy. And rowdy. And a little loud. He asked a lot of questions, too. "Do you like this?" "Does this feel good?" He must have told her a dozen times that she was beautiful, that she was the sexiest woman he'd ever seen. "By leaps and bounds," he said. And he wasn't shy about telling her what he wanted, and exactly how she should do it. "Touch me here, lick me there. Faster. Slower. Just like that." She'd never been with a man so chatty during sex. Or bossy. But the best part by far was watching him reach his peak, seeing him completely let go, knowing that she was the one making him feel that way.

When it was over, and they lay there in a sweaty tangle, she couldn't seem to wipe the smile from her face, until she realized, with considerable horror, that she hadn't given a single freaking thought to birth control.

Luc lay with Julie, his leg resting between hers, one arm under her neck, the other draped across her stomach. "I guess an annulment is out of the question now," he joked, and without warning Julie shot up in bed, nearly dumping him over the edge onto the floor—the *hardwood* floor—and spewed a string of expletives.

Luc sat up beside her. He put a hand on her shoulder and she jumped, as if she'd forgotten he was there. "It was a joke, Julie."

"Oh my God," she said, looking panicked, the color leaching from her face. "I can't believe we did this. How could I be so stupid?"

But it had been some of the best sex he'd ever had, and she had seemed to enjoy herself, too. "Don't you think it's a little late to be having second thoughts?"

She looked puzzled, then said, "I'm not having second thoughts. At least, not in the way you think."

"In what way, then?"

"This is probably a dumb question under the circumstances, but did we just have unprotected sex?"

Is that what this was about? "Relax, you're not going to catch anything from me."

"I know that," she said. "But unless you're sterile, we could have bigger problems."

Whoa, wait a minute. "I thought you were on the Pill. You told me you were."

Her eyes went wide with indignation. "When did I say that? I *never* said that."

"A couple of years ago. You were complaining that it made you nauseous."

"Which is why I *stopped* taking it."

Aw, hell. He should have asked. He was a doctor, after all. He knew better than to assume. Which is why he always kept condoms on hand. They were in the drawer in his bedside table, not two feet away. "This is my fault. I should have checked with you first."

"No, I'm just as much to blame. It never even crossed my mind." She dropped her head in her hands. "How could I be so careless? I don't want a baby. Definitely not now, maybe not ever."

"Before you get all panicked, stop and think about where you are in your cycle."

She took a deep breath, looking so tense she could have snapped like a twig. It took her several seconds to collect herself, then she said, "I'm due to start my period in a couple of days. A week tops."

"Then, we're probably fine. The odds are pretty slim that you would conceive so late in your cycle."

"Is that your official medical opinion?"

"It is." There was a sprinkle of optimism in his tone for good measure. And on the bright side, it wouldn't be long before they knew for sure.

"You're right," she said, sounding a little less freaked out. She rested her head on his shoulder. "I'm sorry I got so upset."

He put his arm around her shoulder, drawing her closer. "No apology required."

She was quiet for a moment, then said, "Just so you know, I don't usually sleep with men on the first date. But since our first date was our wedding, I thought I could make an exception."

"I understand."

She smiled up at him. "That was really good, by the way. The sex, I mean."

"Was?"

She looked confused.

"There is no 'was.'" He lay back and pulled her on top of him. "We're just getting started."

Six

Julie woke slowly the next morning to the sound of water running. Her first thought was that the leaky pipe under her bathroom sink had finally burst. Eyes too heavy to open, she reached over to grab her phone off the bedside table, but it was gone. Not just her phone, but the table itself wasn't there. She pried her eyes open only to realize that this was not her bedroom. Not even her apartment. She lived with Luc now, and the sound of the running water was coming from his bathroom. Then she recalled last night and a smile curled her lips.

Best. Sex. Ever.

She had always assumed, because Luc was so reserved and practical, that he would be the same way in bed. Boy, was she wrong. Hours later she still felt limp as a dishrag and sore in places she didn't know could get sore. If she knew he would be that good she would have jumped him years ago. Just thinking about it was getting her all worked up again. Then she remembered that they forgot to use a condom the first time and her heart sank a little. But Luc was right, the odds were low she would get pregnant. And if she had, they would deal with it. At least they were married. Right?

She sat up and looked around for her phone, finding it in her purse on the floor beside the bed. It was 8:00 a.m., which was early even for her. Sundays were the only days she allowed herself to sleep in. She typically dragged herself out of bed around ten, went for a run around the track at the high school, then showered and sometimes met Lark for brunch. But not today. She looked at the platinum band on the ring finger of her left hand. She was a newlywed. A married woman.

That was going to take some getting used to.

The water shut off, and a minute later she could hear Luc humming to himself—one of those country songs he loved so much—while he shaved. She'd only ever heard him hum when he was in a good mood. And why wouldn't he be after last night?

He would be out of the bathroom any minute now and she really should go to her own room, lest she be tempted to pounce on him. But she wanted to see him. She wrestled with her options, but before she could make a decision, the bathroom door opened and Luc stepped out. And boy was she glad that she stayed. He wore a towel slung low on his hips, his dark hair damp, his face cleanly shaven and smooth. Droplets of water clung to his chest, rolling down his pecs and over those wonderfully ripped abs.

She usually looked like a beast in the morning, her hair askew, pillow creases on her cheek, and she imagined the liner and mascara had smeared under her eyes for that charming raccoon effect, but he'd seen her looking worse.

"Good morning," he said, looking surprised to see her awake.

"G'morning. You're up early."

He shrugged. "Habit."

He was usually at the hospital by 7:00 a.m. to start his rounds, but this was Sunday, not to mention their honeymoon. Technically speaking.

He sat on the edge of the bed beside her and kissed her forehead. If he was put off by her appearance he didn't say so. "Sleep well?"

"Like the dead." When she had finally gotten to sleep, which hadn't been until 3:00 a.m. or so. In typical man style he'd fallen asleep before her, about a half an hour earlier. For a long time she'd lain there wrapped up in his arms, listening to his slow even breaths, wishing they could hit Rewind and relive the night all over again. "How about you? Sleep well?"

"Great. How are you feeling this morning?"

How was she feeling? "A little sore, actually. You gave me quite the workout."

"Jules, I don't mean physically."

She didn't think so. "I'm not having regrets, if that's what you mean. Are you?"

"Nope. I do feel a little guilty for not feeling guilty, if that makes any sense."

"I know exactly what you mean."

"Are you sorry that we can't have a honeymoon?" he asked.

"Not at all. You have responsibilities. We both do. In fact, I was thinking about going into work for a while today."

"You can't."

"Why not?"

"Because I read somewhere that a marriage isn't official unless the newlyweds spend the day after their wedding together."

Oh, so they were going to play this game again. "Did it say what we have to do?"

"We have to have sex again. Then lunch, and maybe a walk in the park. Or we could combine the two and have a picnic, weather permitting."

That sounded like fun. "What then?"

"More sex, of course."

Of course. "And after that?"

"A candlelight dinner."

"Then more sex?"

"Obviously." He shot her one of those steamy smiles. "And we should get started right away. You know, to make it official."

He hooked the edge of the covers and slowly eased them down, revealing her breasts, which were covered in love bites, then her stomach, then the tops of her thighs. *Here we go again*, she thought, struck by how natural it felt. How comfortable she was with him, as if they had been sleeping together all along. And at the same time it felt exciting and new.

His hand, which was still warm from his shower, came to rest on her thigh, then trailed slowly upward, his touch light, it was barely more than a tickle. Her legs parted, giving him space to play around, but they were interrupted by a firm rap on his bedroom door. He mumbled a curse, removed his hand and pulled the covers back up over her.

"I'll make it quick," he said.

He grabbed his robe from the foot of the bed and tugged it on as he walked to the door. Julie sat and held the blanket up to cover herself.

It was his mother's nurse. She glanced over, saw Julie in the bed and quickly averted her eyes. Julie was surprised Luc had opened the door wide enough to let her see inside.

"I'm sorry to bother you, Mr. Wakefield, but I thought you should know that your mother is running a low-grade fever."

A look of concern transformed his face. "How high?"

"Only 99.8. She said that she feels fine, and not to bother you, but I thought you should know."

For the average healthy person a temperature that low wouldn't have been a big deal, but Julie knew that any sign of systemic infection had to be addressed immediately. Elizabeth had barely gotten over the last illness and her body was still weak. Another infection this soon, even something as simple as the common cold could spiral out of control and become deadly.

"Did you check for sores or wounds?" he asked the nurse.

"She wouldn't let me."

Luc sighed and shook his head. "I'll be down there in a minute. And tell her that *I* told you to check her."

"Yes, sir," she said, and he closed the door, mumbling to himself about his mother being stubborn.

Ever look in a mirror? Julie wanted to say.

"You realize she saw me," she told him.

"I know she did." He stepped into his closet for clothes, seemingly unconcerned.

"What if she tells your mother?" Julie called after him.

"So what if she does?" he called back.

"Didn't you tell her that this isn't a real marriage? That we're still just friends."

"I seem to recall you telling me last night that to

make the marriage official we had to have sex." He stepped out wearing jeans and pulling a T-shirt over his head. "Didn't you?"

"You know damn well I made that up to get you into bed. You were being very...uncooperative."

His brows rose. "Is that what I was doing?"

"Don't change the subject. You don't think it will confuse your mother?"

"Her body may be failing her but as you know, her mind is sound."

That was putting it mildly. "I know. I just... I respect her and I don't want her to think I'm slutty."

"For having sex with your husband?"

She shot him a look. "You know what I mean. It might upset her."

"What is she going to do? Ground me? Besides, we're two consenting adults. Married or not, it's still not hers or anyone else's business what we do in bed."

"You know you're impossible."

"I have to go check on her," he said, but he was smiling.

"I'm going to take a shower."

"When I get back we're going to finish what we just started," he said, grinning suggestively as he walked out. If she hadn't already been aroused, that would have definitely done the trick.

She had been a little worried that this morning might be awkward, or involve misplaced guilt and needless justifications. There was nothing more depressing than to wake up with a man and hear why the fantastic sex you had the night before was a mistake. That had happened to her once, and was the precise reason she didn't sleep with men on the first date.

The only thing that seemed to have changed with Luc was that now they both knew what the other looked like naked. *Totally* naked. Up close and *very* personal.

And if he was okay with his mother realizing what was going on between them, who was Julie to question it?

Elizabeth, it turned out, had a small scratch on the back of her thigh that had become infected. Because she had no feeling below the waist, she'd had no idea it was there. Which is why daily physical exams, especially after she'd been moved in and out of her chair frequently, were so critical. With such poor circulation, the smallest scratch could become a festering wound overnight.

Knowing she was bound to get worse before she got better, Luc stayed with her, and they never did get to finish what they'd started. But as she told Beth last night, she didn't expect him to drop everything when she snapped her fingers. Besides, he had just done her an enormous favor; the last thing she had the right to do was demand his attention. In fact, without the threat of deportation looming in the future, this was the most content and happiest she'd felt in months. Any uncertainty she'd had about her future was gone.

She was confident that it would be smooth sailing from here on out.

Luc spent his first day as a husband not in bed having phenomenal sex with his new wife—sex he never planned on having—but instead carefully monitoring his mother's condition. He felt guilty that he'd had to cancel his and Julie's plans, but not only had she not complained, or acted the least bit perturbed, she spent most of the day with him at his mother's bedside. Her temperature continued to rise, slowly but steadily all day, even after the nurse cleaned and dressed her wound and administered ibuprofen and intravenous antibiotics. He was considering hospitalization when finally, around eight that evening, her fever broke. He checked on her several times during the night, and by Monday morning her temperature was holding steady in the normal range and her wound seemed to be healing well.

"I think I need to hire a new nurse," he told Julie that morning. She sat on the edge of his bed, looking adorably mussed, watching him get ready for work. She had offered, for his own peace of mind, to stay home from work and keep an eye on his mother and the nurse. Which was a bit like needing a babysitter to watch the babysitter. "This could have been prevented if she had only done her job. I've stressed to her, more than once, that the physical exams are critical. And my mother knows better. If the nurse can't handle her—"

"Your mother really likes this nurse."

"That isn't my concern." Her safety and physical well-being were the only things that mattered.

"It should be your concern," she said in a tone so sharp it nearly took him back a step. "How would you feel having some stranger inspect every inch of your body twice a day, day in and day out? And don't you think there would be times when you just wanted to say to hell with it and take a break? Maybe her nurse was being more compassionate than negligent. She made a mistake."

He tugged on his shirt and buttoned it, saying, "A mistake that could have cost my mother her life."

"And I'm sure she's learned her lesson."

She damn well better have.

Julie was quiet for a minute, then said, "I've mentioned my nanny Ginise, haven't I?"

"That was the nice one, right?"

"Did I ever tell you why my dad fired her?"

He shook his head, looking thoughtful. "I don't think so."

"I'm sure I told you how strict my father was."

He nodded. From all the stories Julie had told him, to say her father was strict was putting it mildly. She and her sister were practically prisoners in their own home.

"Nanny Ginise was hard-nosed when he was around, but when he was gone, she really loosened the leash. She let me and my sister go to friends' houses and use the phone. She let us go without tights on hot days. She let us drink soda and eat candy. Nanny Ginise gave us the freedom to be kids. Which is eventually what got her fired."

"What happened?"

"One of my friends from school was having a pool party. I begged my father to let me go. All of my friends were going to be there, including boys—though I didn't tell him that—but he still said it was out of the question. I cried and pleaded but he wouldn't budge. But the day of the party he was away on business and wasn't due back until the following night. Nanny Ginise let me go. She even bought me a two-piece bathing suit to wear, since all the other girls would be wearing them and I wanted to fit in. I mean, what thirteen-year-old girl doesn't?"

He flipped his collar up and looped his tie around his neck. "Naturally."

"Well, my father came home early, and Nanny Ginise had no choice but to tell him where I was. He charged over to my friend's house, which was just up the road. The fact that I defied him was bad enough, but when he saw what I was wearing, and that there were boys there, he went ballistic. I had never seen him so furious. He pulled me out of the pool by my hair."

Luc's eyes went wide. "In front of everyone?"

She nodded. "He wrapped me up in a towel and dragged me home. I was mortified, and as if that wasn't punishment enough, I wasn't allowed to leave my room for a month. I was a prisoner. He even made me eat my meals in there."

That wasn't strict, that was abuse. He knew her childhood was bad, but he hadn't realized just how bad. "How could he treat his own children that way?"

"Our mother's death really hit him hard. I'm still not sure if he was trying to shelter us, or if he just resented us."

"Why would he resent you?"

"For being alive, when she wasn't. It took years for me to accept that it wasn't my fault. That it was his problem, not mine."

The idea that she grew up so miserable made his chest ache. "And Nanny Ginise, what happened to her?"

"Fired on the spot. Two days later we had a new nanny. Ms. Fowler, a retired headmistress of a private girls school in Wales."

"What was she like?"

"Horrible. She'd followed our father's rules to the

letter. And came up with quite a few of her own. She believed that teenage girls all had lusty and indecent thoughts and therefore should not be left alone to their own devices. She forbade us from closing our bedroom doors, and walked right in without knocking whenever she felt like it. If she caught us doing something she considered inappropriate she gave us the switch."

"The switch?"

"Yeah, it was this stick she carried around with her all the time."

Luc blinked. "Are you saying that she used to hit you with it?"

"All the time. Damned thing hurt like a bitch and left nasty welts."

Jesus. Luc actually felt sick to his stomach. "Did your father know?"

"Of course. He was all for corporal punishment."

And it just kept getting worse. "Did he hit you?"

"Me *and* my sister. But she got the worst of it. I learned to drop my head, keep my mouth shut and be as invisible as possible. Jennifer was outspoken and defiant. I remember a time, not long before I left for college, when she snuck out of the house in the middle of the night to meet a boy. Our father caught her. There was hardly a spot on her that wasn't black and blue. He grounded her to her room for weeks."

Luc sat down on the bed beside her, at a loss for words. "I don't even know what to say. I knew your childhood wasn't ideal, but I had no idea it was that bad."

"I didn't tell you to make you feel sorry for me. I just want you to try to see things from your mother's point of view. She's a prisoner in a body that constantly betrays her. I think the nurse was just trying to cut her a little slack, like Nanny Ginise did for me and my sister. There was no malicious intent. And I know she feels horrible about it."

Wow, talk about a convincing argument, and she spoke of it so matter-of-factly, as if it had happened to someone else. And yes, sometimes he forgot what his mother must go through. How difficult and unpleasant her life could be. Years ago, before her surgery, she was active and independent. Now she relied on others for most of her needs. That couldn't be easy for her. "You're right," he told Julie. "She meant no harm. If my mother is happy with her, then I'm happy."

"Thank you. You're a good man. And an even better son."

"I don't know about that," he said.

She smiled. "I do."

He couldn't help himself. He had to kiss her. He leaned in and she met him halfway. He was enjoying this arrangement, and found himself thinking about her, far more than he should have.

The kiss didn't last long. Julie patted his shoulders and said, "You need to get to the hospital. You'll be late for rounds."

She was right. Typically he looked forward to work, but today staying home in bed with Julie sounded much more fun. "Maybe tonight, if all goes well—"

"Yes," she said with a saucy smile, knowing exactly what he was going to say before he said it. It looked as if he wasn't the only one with sex on the brain. And if he didn't finish getting dressed and get his ass out of there, he might not make it to the hospital at all. It had been a long time since he'd been so hot for a woman he wanted to play hooky from work.

He stood, knotting his tie, then pulled on his suit jacket. She sat on the bed watching him. "Are you sure you're okay with staying home today?"

"I have my laptop," she said. "I can work here. I have some numbers to crunch. And phone calls to make. And your mom mentioned something about a few rounds of poker."

"For God's sake don't let her talk you into playing for money."

Julie laughed. "She's a cardsharp, I know."

"And she's ruthless."

He grabbed his wallet and keys from the basket on the chest of drawers, hesitating another second. Damn, he really didn't want to go. If it weren't for the new patient he was seeing this morning, he just might stick around for a while, have one of his residents do rounds for him.

"I'll see you tonight," he said. He considered kissing her goodbye, but once he got started he wouldn't want to stop. "Call me if there's a problem."

"I will."

He was almost to the door when Julie said, "Hey, Luc."

He turned to find her kneeling on his bed. Then she dropped the covers to flash him.

Her breasts were full and firm. Not large by modern standards, but they fit her just right and he couldn't wait to get his hands on them again.

With that saucy smile, she said, "Have a nice day, dear."

Oh, he definitely would. And an even better night.

Seven

Luc made it to work with five minutes to spare, stopping in the cafeteria for a cup of coffee on his way up to his office.

"Cutting it close today," his secretary, Ruth, said, looking at the clock. She was used to him being on time, or most days, a little early.

"Busy weekend," he told her.

"I'll bet. It was a lovely wedding. You two looked so happy, and so in love."

It sounded as if they'd done a pretty good job fooling everyone. But the happy part? That was real. His best friend was here to stay. What more could he ask for?

"Tommy James was admitted last night," she said.

"No problems?"

"Not that I've heard."

"How is the rest of my day looking?" He was hoping to get home at a decent hour tonight. Maybe even a little early. One of his favorite upscale restaurants had reopened in the past week and he thought maybe he would take Julie for a nice dinner.

Oh hell, who was he kidding. To heck with dinner. He wanted to get her back in bed and finish what they'd started.

He shrugged out of his suit jacket. Ruth took it from him and handed him his lab coat. "You have a procedure at 9:15, and a staff meeting at 11:30. In the afternoon you have several consultations. And a meeting at 5:00."

He pulled it on and she clipped his ID onto the pocket. It had been their morning routine for as long as he'd been chief of surgery. A position that was as much about politics as it was medicine. Ruth, who had been in hospital administration for three decades, had been his saving grace.

"So how does it feel?" she asked him, straightening his collar.

Puzzled, he asked, "How does what feel?"

"Being *married.*"

Better than he thought it would. In fact, it was pretty damned fantastic so far. Friendship and sex without the complications. Who wouldn't want that? And it was really good sex.

No, it was *fantastic* sex. And he couldn't wait to get home so they could do it again.

"It's good," he said, and left it at that. "If Julie calls, page me immediately. My mother had an infection over the weekend. Julie is staying with her today."

Ruth clucked and shook her head. "I'm so sorry. I noticed at the wedding that she looked tired. Poor Elizabeth, she's been through so much."

And every infection seemed to suck more of her strength, more of her spirit. As a physician, he knew her time was running out. Her body could handle only so much before it gave out for good. But as her son, he wanted her to live forever.

"She pushes herself too hard," Luc said.

"She's a proud woman."

More stubborn than proud if you asked him.

Luc left his office and checked on the five surgical patients in his care, each in different stages of recovery. Knowing the parents would have a million questions for him, as he would if his son were going in for major surgery, he saved Tommy James in the pediatrics ward for last.

The boy had come in as a referral from a colleague in Houston that Luc had known since med school.

"This is right up your alley," he'd told Luc when he called last week. The five-year-old had congenital lumbar spinal stenosis that had begun to cause him considerable pain, and in the past few weeks he had begun to lose feeling in his legs. It was a rare condition for a child but using techniques he'd perfected himself, with Julie's help of course, Luc could correct the problem by fusing the spine. The parents would be hard-pressed to find a physician more qualified than him to do the surgery.

Because it was congenital, this was quite possibly a temporary fix. As Tommy matured, the stenosis, which started in his lumbar spine, could gradually work its way upward into the thoracic, then cervical spine. This might be one of several surgeries he would need to stabilize his spine before adulthood. But other than his back being less flexible, he would live a long, productive life. Just not as a gymnast. And he would have the bonus of impeccable posture.

Luc stopped outside the patient's door, where a nurse stood updating his chart on her laptop.

"Is he all settled in?"

"Yes, Doctor. He was pretty uncomfortable so I gave

him pain meds. He's sleeping now and his vitals are good. He seems like a real trooper. He always has a smile on his face, even through the pain."

Kids were resilient. It was the parents who were typically the toughest to deal with. "Are the parents in there?"

"His mother stepped out to get coffee. She should be back in a minute."

"And his father?" Luc asked.

"Not here. And from the sound of it, he won't be coming to Royal."

"That's a shame." Luc knew that having a chronically ill child could devastate the soundest of marriages. He'd seen it all too often. But to not be there for your child who's having major surgery? What sort of man was this boy's father?

Though he had studied the chart thoroughly, he gave it another quick look to be sure that nothing had changed before he stepped into the boy's room.

He was indeed asleep, and though he looked small and fragile—all skin and bones—his color was good. Luc checked his vitals again, then he eased him onto his side to see his back, and checked his feet. Despite the loss of feeling in his legs, his circulation was still adequate. There wouldn't be any permanent damage.

He heard someone behind him and turned, his usual greeting on the tip of his tongue and ready to go…then froze when he saw the woman standing there.

The spark of recognition was instantaneous, but it took another ten seconds to determine that his mind wasn't playing tricks on him. That it really was his ex-fiancée, Amelia, standing there holding a cup of coffee and a gossip magazine. The woman who'd shredded his heart like confetti and ate it for breakfast without batting an eyelash.

"Amelia," he said, more a statement than a question, and regretted it the instant the words were out of his mouth. But it was too late now.

She flashed him a weak, tired smile. "Hello, Lucas. How have you been?"

Meeting new patients could be hit-or-miss, yet of the dozens of scenarios he might have imagined, this one didn't even come close to making the list.

She hadn't really changed all that much. She was a little thicker around the middle, and a little older. The stress of her son's condition showed in her face, in the fine lines at the corners of her eyes.

For a good ten seconds he was at a loss for words.

You're the physician, he reminded himself. The one with the upper hand. And she was just the mother of the patient. Nothing more. He had to keep this professional. Yet he heard himself saying, "Should I assume this isn't a coincidence?"

"Yes and no. Tommy's doctor in Houston told me that he knew another doctor with more experience in this sort of surgery. I had already made the decision to come when he told me who and where the doctor was located. Of course then I knew it was you."

"And you came anyway?"

"It's not about me."

She was right. Nor was it about him. And he had no right to question her motives.

Keep it professional. "Why don't we talk about the surgery."

"Okay."

He went into surgeon mode, describing the procedure and recovery in layman's terms, feeling a bit like a robot. It was the same speech he'd used countless times before, but now it felt stilted and awkward.

"His doctor explained all of this in great detail," Amelia said. "He said permanent paralysis was a possibility."

"That is a possibility, but given your son's age, and the fact that he's in otherwise good health, I don't foresee any complications," he said.

Of course there were no guarantees. Complications could arise, but Luc was confident the surgery would go smoothly. Besides, she didn't have much choice at this point. "No surgery comes without risks. But without the procedure, the spinal column will continue to narrow. Then you'll be looking at paralysis, loss of bladder and bowel function. Excessive pain."

"I know all that," she said, looking conflicted. "I just needed to hear it from you. Of course he needs the surgery. And I trust that you'll take good care of him. How soon can you do it?" she asked.

"It would be next week at the soonest."

Her mouth fell open, eyes went wide. He knew that look as well as if he had seen it yesterday. "*Next week?* But he's in pain! I assumed you would do it right away."

He sighed quietly. That was Amelia, always expecting things to be done her way. "I'm already booked up this week and most of next. I have to check with my secretary, but I think I can squeeze it in either next Thursday or the following Tuesday."

"You can't do it *any* sooner?"

"Thursday or Tuesday. That's the best I can do."

She nodded slowly and said with a weak smile, "So, no special treatment for the ex-fiancée, huh?"

Is that what she'd expected? Special treatment? "I have a busy schedule," he told her. "Until the surgery we can control the pain and at this point there's no danger of permanent damage. But he will have to stay in the hospital so we can monitor him."

"If that's the case I'm staying here with him. In the room," she said, her chin lifting a notch, as if she were trying to challenge his authority, when there was really no need. This combative attitude was unnecessary. As her son's surgeon, his patient was his main priority.

"You'll have to talk to your son's nurse about hospital policy," he told her. "But I'm sure it won't be a problem."

"There is something else I wanted to ask you, that, uncomfortable as it is, I feel needs addressing."

He made a point of checking the time on his watch. He was already running late. "Okay."

"I need to be sure, because of our past, that you don't see this as a conflict of interest," she said.

Several years ago it might have been. But after getting over the initial shock of seeing her again, the only thing he felt was a medical obligation to care for his patient to the best of his ability. As he always did.

And she was nothing more to him than the mother of his patient.

"There's no conflict," he said, and he could see the instant she noticed the ring on his left hand.

"Oh. You're married," she said, sounding surprised.

"Yes, I am."

"Anyone I know?"

"No."

She paused, as if she was expecting him to give her

a name, or details, and when he didn't, her smile wavered. "I'm very happy for you.

"In case you're wondering, I'm divorced now. For almost two years. He traded me in for a younger model," she said, bitterness dripping from her words. "They moved to San Antonio and are expecting a baby. He sends Tommy gifts, and calls occasionally, but he never comes to see him."

None of Luc's business. He was her son's doctor, not a confidant.

He checked his watch. "Is there anything else—?"

"Leaving you was the biggest mistake I ever made," she blurted.

Oh, what he would have given to hear those words six years ago, but it was too late to turn back. He was happy with his life just the way it was. He didn't love her anymore. He hadn't for a long time. Maybe all along he'd only been in love with the idea of her, and deep down she had never been what he needed.

Julie was, though. And he did need her. More than he'd ever realized.

"I'll talk to my secretary and see about scheduling the surgery," he told Amelia. "In the meantime I'd like to run some tests."

She looked up at him with big blue eyes that used to melt him on the spot, and he felt nothing. Not a single damn thing. He was beginning to wonder what he had *ever* seen in her. Had he changed so much since then?

It was clear now that all these years he'd been wondering what-if had been a waste of time. Now he knew. Even if she hadn't dumped him, he seriously doubted they would have lasted very long. Her narcissism would have eventually driven him away.

"You don't want to talk about it," she said. "I get it. Just let me say that I'm really sorry for the way things turned out. I know I hurt you. I hope someday you can forgive me."

He might have laughed if he wasn't so appalled. Same old Amelia, thinking she was the center of the universe, and he refused to take the bait.

"I'm ordering tests today. I'll let you know when I get the results." Or more likely, he would tell one of his residents, who would then notify her. The less contact he had with her the better.

"I really am sorry," she said softly, looking genuinely apologetic, but she was six years too late. He turned and walked out without another word.

Julie set up a folding table and chair to make a small work space for herself at the foot of Elizabeth's bed where she could keep an eye on her while the nurse, who had been up most of the night, took a few hours to nap. Luc had spared no expense on his mother's home care. The room was as efficient and well equipped as any hospital room Julie had ever seen, yet it lacked that sterile atmosphere that was inevitable in a hospital setting. But if his mother's health continued to fail her, Luc would have to consider hiring another nurse for the overnight shift.

As fragile as Elizabeth was now, Julie was a little nervous being even temporarily in charge of her care. She was too emotionally invested in the relationship to be impartial. Elizabeth was her mother-in-law, but more than that, she was becoming a good friend. A bit like the mother that Julie never had.

When Julie and Luc first discussed their childhoods,

she had asked him about growing up without a father. Did he feel resentful or cheated? Had he ever wished his mother had remarried?

My mother gave me everything I could have possibly needed, he'd said. *We took care of each other.*

They still did. Julie wished she could have been so fortunate, that there had been someone in her life who always had her back, who loved her unconditionally. Wasn't that what everyone wanted? What everyone needed to feel whole? Luc had brought her closer to that feeling than anyone in her life ever had.

"Are you in love with my son?"

The sound of Elizabeth's voice startled her. She looked up from her laptop and saw that her mother-in-law was watching her. "You're awake. How do you feel?"

The older woman's shoulders lifted in a shrug and she smiled weakly. "Eh, I've been worse."

Her strength of character, her resilience, never ceased to amaze Julie. She could only hope that faced with similar circumstances, she would handle her condition with equal poise.

"So? Are you in love with my son?" she asked again.

"He's the most important person in my life."

"But that isn't what I asked, is it?"

Julie hesitated. Luc was right, his mother was sharp as a tack. "Elizabeth—"

She held a hand up to stop her. "No, no. You don't have to explain. You feel what you feel. I know how that is. But a mother can hope, can't she?"

Julie picked her chair up and moved it closer to Elizabeth's bed. "I'm honored that you feel that way, that you would want me in your son's life, and I wish things were different. I really do. What Luc and I have is very special, it's just not…" She struggled for the words to explain.

"Luc was my miracle baby," Elizabeth said. "Did I ever tell you that?"

Julie shook her head.

Elizabeth smiled wistfully. "His father and I had been trying for five years to have a child."

"Wow, that's a long time." For her and Luc's dad it must have felt like forever.

"Back then there weren't as many options as there are now, but we did everything we could. I was young enough to keep trying, but Luc's father was seventeen years older than me. He felt as if he was getting too old. I was his second wife and he had two grown boys when I met him, so he'd been through it all before. I couldn't blame him for his feelings. But, as these things sometimes happen, when we finally made the decision to give up, when I resigned myself to the fact that I would never have a child of my own, I got pregnant."

"Luc doesn't really talk about his father."

"He doesn't remember him. But they're so very much alike. My husband was a simple man. He believed in hard work and family, and giving back to the community."

"That does sound like Luc."

"We used to own one of the largest ranches in the county. He always hoped his boys from his first marriage would want to take over, but they had no interest in the family business. Or me for that matter. That ranch was his life and out of respect I wanted to keep it running, keep it in the family, but then I had my surgery and everything changed. I couldn't keep up with the day-to-day operations, and like Luc had no interest in ranching. I knew he was meant for greater things. The proceeds from the sale of the business paid for medical school."

"Luc said his dad had a heart attack."

"A massive coronary," she said, looking so sad, even all this time later. "They found him out in the field, his horse at his side. They told me that it was instantaneous, that he never suffered. I always took comfort in the fact that he died doing what he loved most.

"That's why I believe in seizing the moment. Living as though every day might be your last."

"I was in love once," she told Elizabeth. "I met him at university. I thought he was the love of my life."

"But he wasn't?"

She shook her head, the pain of that time still as real and sharp as a slap in the face.

Elizabeth frowned. "If you're uncomfortable talking about it…"

"It's not that," Julie said. It was just embarrassing to admit she had been so desperate for love. So gullible.

"You have to bear in mind how I was raised," she told Elizabeth. "I had no positive male influence in my life. My sister and I grew up believing that nothing we ever did was good enough."

"Oh, honey," Elizabeth said, patting her arm. "You've done amazing things with your life. You've dedicated yourself to helping people. You should be proud of your accomplishments. No matter what anyone else thinks."

That was easier said than done. "I try, but there's always that small part of me that says it's not enough.

That I could be doing more. That I'll never quite measure up."

"Inner demons," Elizabeth said with a sigh. "There's nothing more difficult to face than your own overinflated expectations. Believe me, I've been there."

Julie certainly had her share of those. "I found most men intimidating at that time, but there was something so different about him. He was so gentle and kind. He filled a place in my heart that had been empty for so long. I was able to set my fears aside. I was convinced he would never hurt me. At first."

"But he did."

She nodded. "Things started to gradually change. Little things at first. He became more critical and more demanding. He wanted all of my attention. He resented my friends, my professors, my homework. But I was so desperate for someone to love me, to accept me, I was blind to what was happening, to the way he was gradually tearing down my self-esteem, shrinking my world until I was totally dependent on him. By the end, he controlled nearly every aspect of my life."

"Love makes us do foolish things," Elizabeth said, and something in her eyes said she was speaking from experience. "Especially when we're vulnerable. The important thing is that you got away."

"It took every bit of courage I had to walk away from him. I was miserable for months. He had me convinced that I needed him. But as time passed and things moved into perspective, I was disgusted with myself, and embarrassed that I let it go as far as it did. I felt as if I should have known better. The first time he called me stupid I should have walked out the door." She paused, shaking her head. "No, not walked. I should have run for dear life."

"It's not your fault," Elizabeth said. "You were vulnerable and he took advantage of you. He was a predator."

"And he was damned good at it. I haven't been in a serious relationship since. I still don't trust my own instincts."

"Do you trust Lucas?"

"I do." With her life. He was the only person she trusted unconditionally

"You believe he would never hurt you?"

She could see where Elizabeth was going with this, and though Julie hated to disappoint her, there was no way around it. "Not purposely, no. But Luc and I will never be anything but friends. I love him. I can't imagine what I would do without him. Hands down he's the most important person in my life."

"I know he feels the same way about you."

That didn't change anything. "I'm sure as a mother, you want what's best for Luc," Julie said.

"Of course."

"Even if we were in love, he deserves someone without all the emotional baggage. It would be unfair to lay that all on him."

"Everyone has emotional baggage, Julie. *Everyone*. Even Luc."

Yes, well, some had more than others. Elizabeth didn't realize that Julie was doing both her and Luc a favor. She didn't know the first thing about being a wife. Or a daughter-in-law, for that matter.

"I wish things were different. I don't doubt that Luc would be an exceptional husband. In fact, I *know* he would be. It's my role as his wife that I'm not so confident about."

"Shouldn't Luc be the one to make that decision?"

As far as Julie was concerned, he already had. "I can't force myself to fall in love, and neither can he."

Eight

The nurse returned from her nap a few minutes later to check Elizabeth's vitals and gently suggested that it was time for her to rest. Julie gathered her things and went back to her bedroom, where she set up a work area at the small desk under the window overlooking the rolling green lawns and sprouting flower beds of the estate.

She opened the window and breathed in deeply. Spring was in the air. When she'd arrived in October, everywhere she looked there was devastation. It seemed as if now, slowly but surely, the town was waking up to the world, and life in Royal was returning to normal. Or what she perceived to be normal. Displaced families were back in their homes, and every week shops and restaurants had begun reopening.

She needed to get out more and explore the city. If this was to be her permanent home, she needed to get to know it better. And the people. That was the worst part of growing up so sheltered. The lack of community, missing that feeling of belonging somewhere. But things were different now. *She* was different.

She smiled to herself, thinking, *This is home*. This was exactly where she was meant to be.

Taking one last deep breath of cool fresh air, she closed the window, opened her laptop and got back to work. Sorting data took every bit of her attention and concentration, so it was no surprise that she didn't hear Luc walk in the room. When he spoke her name, she nearly jumped out of her skin.

"Didn't mean to startle you," he said, but he knew as well as she that when she was immersed in work, startling her was inevitable. "How's the research going?"

"Great." She looked over at the clock, surprised to see that it was barely after four. She couldn't remember the last time he'd left the hospital before seven in the evening.

Her first thought was that something must have been wrong. "Is everything okay?"

"Fine," he said, shrugging out of his jacket, which he then tossed over the footboard of her bed. "Why wouldn't it be?"

"The time, for one. You're home so early."

He loosened his tie and pulled it off, then started unfastening the buttons on his dress shirt. "I told Ruth to clear my afternoon. That I had something I needed to do."

Something that required he take his clothes off, because that's what he was doing. And why was her bedroom door closed? "What do you need to do?"

A sexy grin tipped up the corners of his lips. "You, of course."

What the advance lacked in creativity, he made up for with red-hot sex appeal. He unbuttoned his shirt, slowly exposing a band of smooth, defined chest with just a sprinkle of crisp black hair.

Nice.

"You know, I almost stopped to pick up Mardi Gras beads on the way home," he said.

Huh? Why would they need those?

Seeing her confused look, he said, "You don't recall flashing me this morning?"

Oh yes, she had done that, hadn't she. She never dreamed that a quick peek at her breasts in the morning would motivate him to cancel his afternoon appointments and rush home three hours early.

Damn. She must be doing something right.

"We never had our postwedding sex-a-thon. Unless you don't want to," he teased, his shirt halfway down his arms. Big, thick, delicious arms she wanted to feel wrapped around her.

"Oh, I want to," she said.

"Then, why are you sitting over there?" he asked, and the hunger in his eyes made her heart flutter.

"I'm enjoying the view."

"You'll enjoy it more on the bed."

She'd never known him to be impatient, but rather than wait for her to get up on her own, he walked over to her chair and scooped her up, then tossed her onto the bed.

He did seem to enjoy manhandling her, and weirdly enough, she liked it.

Bare chested and beautiful, Luc climbed up with her, kneeling on the mattress, straddling her thighs. "So, about this shirt."

She looked down at the totally unsexy but comfortable T-shirt she'd thrown on this morning. "What about it?"

"It needs to go."

No problem. She made a move to pull it over her head, but he said, "Allow me."

He grabbed the front of her shirt in his fists and gave it one good tug. She gasped as the fabric came apart in his hands.

"Better," he said, looking satisfied with himself. He was literally tearing her clothes off. And she *liked* it.

He unfastened her jeans and tugged them off, though she had the feeling that if he could have torn the denim, he probably would have ripped those off of her, too. But now he was eyeing her bra, and thank goodness for the front clasp or he may have tried to rip that off, too.

Of course the panties were the next to go. Had she been wearing socks he would no doubt rip those, as well.

Luc sat back to admire his work. "You're perfect," he said, his eyes raking over her. He cupped her breasts, rolling her nipple between his thumb and forefinger. He knew from their wedding night how crazy that made her.

"Tell me what you like," he said, pinching hard enough to make her gasp. "I'll do anything."

"Anything. Everything." *Just keep touching me.*

His brow lifted. *"Anything?"*

The look in her eyes must have said it all. She wasn't sure what she was getting herself into, but she didn't care. In the past she never would have suggested such a thing. She would never leave herself so exposed. The ramifications would have scared her to death. Amazing what trust could do.

And boy did he "do" her. And kept on doing her.

For two solid hours. Until he'd established an up-close-and-personal relationship with every inch of her body.

"I need to rest," she finally said, limp and draped across the bed, her head hanging over the side of the mattress. The comforter lay on the floor, the bottom sheet had come loose and was halfway off, and the top sheet was…well, she wasn't sure where that had gone.

"Finished *already*?" he asked, but his smile said he was teasing her.

"Aren't you supposed to roll over and go to sleep?" she said.

"You don't want me to do that."

She did and she didn't.

Her stomach rumbled and she realized that not only was it dinnertime, but she'd skipped lunch today.

"No more sex until you feed me," she said.

"We could go out. We never did get that candlelit dinner I promised you."

"Would I have to get up and get dressed?"

"I highly recommend it."

That sounded romantic and all, but putting on clothes and fixing her hair was just too darned much work. "Or we can make sandwiches and eat in bed."

"Are you sure you don't want to go out?" he asked, looking as if he was still raring to go. Did he ever get tired?

Her legs were so weak from being overextended—she hadn't realized her feet could go that far over her head—she wouldn't make it to the front door. "Some other time."

"Sandwiches it is," he said, hopping off the bed. *He actually hopped.* Then he pulled his slacks back on, walked to the door and, wiggling his eyebrows suggestively, said, "I'll be back. Don't start without me."

Not a chance.

She must have dozed off, because he was back in what seemed like seconds, a tray propped on one palm.

"Dinner is served," he said, setting it right on the bed.

She dragged herself into a sitting position, noticing that he was hiding something behind his back. "Whatcha got?"

"Let's call it dessert."

"Can I see what it is?"

He held up a squeeze bottle of chocolate syrup, wearing that lascivious grin, and all she could think was, *Oh boy, here we go again.*

The rest of the week flew by. Luc and Julie tried to make time for one another, but life kept getting in the way. Luc had hoped to spend Sunday with Julie, but she had already promised Megan she would volunteer for the pet adoption fair, to find homes for the animals displaced in the storm.

The following Monday Luc was sitting in the cafeteria catching up on his reading while he ate a late lunch, when someone sat down across the table from him. He glanced up from the medical journal, expecting to see a colleague sitting there.

It was Amelia.

He cursed silently. He had no other patients in Pediatric, and hadn't seen her since the consultation last Monday. To be honest, he hadn't given her much thought, either. But that hadn't stopped her from seeking him out. She'd come to his office several times hoping to "catch him" and he heard that she'd objected rather firmly when his resident came to check in on Tommy in Luc's place.

As careful as he'd been to avoid her, here she was anyway, invading his space. Other than information about her son's care, he had nothing to say to her.

"Someone has been avoiding me," she said in a sing-song tone. Her smile said she thought she was being cute, when in reality, it was just annoying.

"Is there something I can help you with?"

Her smile wavered. "I saw you sitting here so I thought I would stop and say hi."

"Hi," he replied, knowing that wouldn't be the end of it. He recognized that determined look on her face.

"It would be nice if we could talk."

Nice for her maybe. As far as he was concerned they had nothing to say to each other. "I have an extremely busy afternoon."

"You know you can't stay mad at me forever, Luc."

He wasn't mad, just disinterested in whatever she had to say. She seemed hell-bent on getting him to concede his feelings, but the truth was, he didn't have any. At least, not the kind she expected him to have. "As Tommy's surgeon, it's critical that I remain impartial. I'm sure you can understand."

"I just want to talk," she said. "I've missed you. Haven't you missed me even the tiniest little bit?"

His blank expression had her frowning.

"You're playing the tough guy. I get it."

"I'm not *playing* anything," he said. "I'm just trying to eat my lunch in peace."

"No need to get snippy," she said, in the voice one

might use while addressing an impatient child. "I'm just trying to be polite."

Had she used that tone with him six years ago? And if she had, how did he stand it?

He looked across the table at her. *Really looked.* He wondered what it was about her that he had found so appealing. She was attractive, in a debutante sort of way. Never a hair out of place, her makeup applied to perfection, her clothes designer and expensive. And he had been a penniless college student, working two jobs, struggling to keep up with her high expectations. Which seemed ridiculous now when he considered the generous weekly allowance her father provided. And if that wasn't enough, all she had to do was ask and he would supply her with yet another credit card.

Her parents thought that Luc, the lowly son of a rancher, wasn't good enough for their precious daughter. But Luc knew he was destined for great things, and he was proud of all that he'd accomplished. He wondered what her parents would think of him now, and realized he didn't really give a damn. But he sure had back then. Amelia wanted the prestigious role of a surgeon's wife, but not the work and sacrifice it would take to get there. But like any other young resident he'd had to pay his dues, and Amelia had no patience to wait around for him.

"So, how is your mother?" she asked him. "I heard that she's been ill."

"She's recovering."

"She must get lonely in that big house all by herself. Maybe I could come visit her someday."

Not a good idea. His mother never liked Amelia. *That girl is too big for her britches*, she used to say.

There was nothing his mother liked less than pretension, and Amelia's nose was—as his mother liked to say—locked in an upright position. His mother's wheelchair made Amelia feel awkward, as if by going anywhere near it she might catch something.

In all the time he'd dated her, he couldn't recall Amelia and his mother having any more than a five-minute conversation. So why the need to talk to her now? And what did she know about his "big house"? Had she been snooping into his personal life?

He wondered where he would be now if she hadn't run off with someone else. He'd been too proud to beg her to come back, but he'd wanted to. Those first few months afterward he'd been beside himself. It was only after he met Julie that he began to feel whole again. She was the one who filled the empty place in his heart. Just by being a good friend.

"My mother isn't well enough for visitors," he told Amelia. "Her immune system is too vulnerable."

"I'm sorry to hear that," Amelia said. "Maybe some other time."

Doubtful.

"Please send her my regards."

When he was away from work, Amelia was the furthest thing from his mind. And why would he think about her when he had Julie? Even though they weren't a real couple, she was everything he could ask for in a woman, and a wife. And especially a lover. Pleasing her, making her feel good, was by far his favorite part of the day. There was only one thing missing. After sex, she always went back to her own room to sleep. If he had his way, she would be sleeping in his bed. Even if it was only temporarily.

"Just the man I wanted to see," Luc heard some-one say, and turned to see Drew walking toward him, swooping in like an angel of mercy to save him. He looked from Luc to Amelia, one brow raised slightly. "I hope I'm not interrupting."

"Not at all," Luc said, pushing to his feet, picking up the tray with his half-eaten lunch. "I'm finished."

With his lunch *and* with Amelia. He didn't introduce her to Drew, nor did he say goodbye when he walked away. Maybe now, after this chilly conversation, she would take the hint and leave him alone.

He dumped the contents of his tray in the trash on their way out of the cafeteria and asked Drew, "What brings you to the hospital?"

"I dropped off fresh flowers at the gift shop for Beth, then came in here for a soda. Then I saw you and, frankly, you looked like maybe you needed rescuing."

Now, that was a true friend. "Drew, you have no idea."

They stopped at the main bank of elevators. "Is that her?"

"Is that who?"

"Your ex."

Luc blinked. He'd made it a point not to say any-thing to anyone about Amelia's being in Royal. Not even Julie. "How did you know she was my ex?"

"Amelia…is that her name?"

Luc nodded.

"Well, she's been kinda broadcasting it all over town."

Disbelief stopped him in his tracks. "She's doing *what*?"

"Word is spreading fast."

Fantastic. Just what he needed. But was he surprised? Not really. Amelia loved to be the center of attention. And he'd bet anything she was pinning him as the bad guy. "What has she been saying?"

"She's making like you guys are getting chummy. At least, that's what I've heard."

He cursed and shook his head. "Nothing could be further from the truth. Today was the first I've seen of her in a week. And it wasn't by choice, believe me."

"Yeah, you looked pretty uncomfortable sitting there with her. What does Julie think about her being here?"

"Like I said, I haven't told anyone."

Drew looked pained. "Please, tell me you're joking."

"I prefer to leave work at work. Amelia is the mother of my patient, nothing more. She has nothing to do with my personal life."

Drew's expression said that Luc was a sad and pathetic man. "Dude, I hate to be the one to break it to you, but in a marriage, it doesn't really work that way."

"But we're not really married, are we?"

"No, but she is your best friend. I thought you guys told each other everything."

Well, almost everything. And he could see Drew's point. If Amelia was broadcasting the details of their past relationship, Julie was bound to hear it from someone. He didn't want it to appear as if he was hiding things from her. "I'll talk to her tonight."

"Smart move. The way it's spreading, it's only a matter of time before the entire town knows."

Luc cursed under his breath. He should have known that Amelia was up to something. He should have expected it.

Hadn't she done enough damage? Caused him enough pain. He was going to put an end to whatever she thought she was doing.

Nine

Julie met Megan and Lark for lunch at the Royal Diner. There was a real camaraderie among the three of them, a sense of genuine respect and friendship. Only recently, as she'd grown so close to these women, did Julie realize all that she'd missed out on being so sheltered as a child, and having that inherent lack of trust. But it was never too late to start living.

"The adoption fair seemed to go well," she told Megan after the waitress took their orders.

"And we're still bursting at the seams. It's like that every spring, plus we're still feeling the aftereffects of the tornado. We have a lot of animals coming in, but not so many getting adopted back out. I don't suppose you would be interested in a puppy or a kitten? Or better yet an older cat or dog?"

Julie had never had a pet before. Her father forbade animals of any kind in the house, and at university, with a full class-load, there hadn't been time. After that she'd moved around so frequently, spending months abroad, owning an animal, even something as benign as a goldfish, had been impractical.

Her condo in Royal had a no-pet policy, so adopting had never been an option. But she no longer had that obstacle, did she? She wondered how Luc would feel about adopting a small dog or even a cat. He spoke fondly of the various pets his family had owned in their ranching days, so she knew he liked animals.

"Maybe I'll come by and take a look," she said. "After I talk to Luc about it, of course."

"Speaking of," Megan said. "How is he holding up?"

"He's good." It had been touch and go with his mother all last week, but now she was infection free, eating better than she had in months and growing stronger every day. As they drew closer to April, and the days grew warmer, Elizabeth had been spending time outside in the gardens with her nurse.

"It must have been a shock for him," Lark said.

"Not really," Julie told her. "It's just a part of her condition."

"Condition?" Megan asked, looking confused. "I thought her son was the patient. Is Luc treating her, too? And wouldn't that be a conflict of interest?"

Julie frowned. *Her* who?

"Far as I heard he's only treating the boy," Lark said. "Which is bad enough if you ask me."

There were obviously some crossed wires here. "I'm a little confused."

"And that's perfectly natural," Megan said. "I would be, too, if Drew's ex showed up."

Drew's ex? *Wait, what?*

Before she could ask what the heck they were talking about, she noticed Stella approaching their table.

"Hello, ladies! Isn't this fantastic." She gazed around the diner. "It's so inspiring to see things getting back to normal in our little town."

"Are you here for lunch?" Lark asked her.

"Would you like to join us?" Megan chimed in. "We're giving Julie some much needed moral support."

They were? And what exactly did she need support for?

Stella sat in the empty chair next to Julie and with eyes full of sympathy said, "I heard she was in town. How are *you* holding up?"

She who? "Guys, I'm really confused."

"Of course you are," Stella said gently. "Who wouldn't be under the circumstances."

"No, I mean I'm confused right now, by this conversation. I must have missed something, because I'm lost. Who are we talking about?"

"Amelia," Stella said.

"Amelia who?" The only Amelia that she knew of was the one who'd broken Luc's heart. The one he was still hung up on all these years later. They couldn't possibly mean...

The three women exchanged a look, and Megan said, "I'm sorry. We just assumed Luc had told you."

Julie was beginning to get a very bad feeling. "Told me what?"

"His ex-fiancée, Amelia. Her son is Luc's patient."

Amelia was here, in Royal? Julie's stomach did an odd little flip-flop and a rush of heat flooded her cheeks.

As his wife, she should have known that. Even as his fake wife, a heads-up would have been nice. Weren't they supposed to make this marriage look legitimate?

"I guess it must have slipped his mind," Julie said. Though technically Luc was her boss, it wasn't often that their paths crossed at the hospital. On the average day, she rarely left her office. And though she had seen a picture of Amelia from six years ago, she had no clue what she would look like now. She could have passed her in the hall and not even known it. "We're both pretty busy. Some nights we don't even see each other."

Maybe Amelia and her son had just arrived and he'd forgotten to mention it. And maybe seeing her again, talking things over with her, would give him the closure he needed. So really, this could be a good thing. Right?

"When did she get here?" Julie asked them, forcing a smile, trying her best not to come off as the jilted wife.

The women exchanged another look and the bad feeling grew.

"Last Monday," Stella said.

For reasons that escaped her, Julie's heart plummeted to the pit of her belly and her appetite disappeared. She had been in Royal for more than a week?

"I'm so sorry you had to find out this way," Lark said. "We all just assumed you knew."

As Luc's wife, she should have known. But as his friend and employee, since that's all they really were, he was under no obligation to tell her anything. He had his life and she had hers. But he'd put her in a difficult situation.

She wracked her brain for a way to backpedal, to make herself look at least a little less pathetic, but trying to explain something she had no real answer for would only make things worse. Maybe Luc was trying to protect her feelings, or maybe he figured she wouldn't care either way.

You're rationalizing, and for no good reason, she told herself. It was what it was. An arrangement. After all that he'd done for her, how could she complain? If he wanted to talk about it with her he would in his own good time. And if he didn't, that was okay, too.

"He probably just didn't want to upset you," Megan said. "Her showing up so soon after the wedding. Maybe he felt hesitant to tell you."

"Or maybe he's so over her that he didn't feel the need to say anything," Lark added.

Julie appreciated their efforts, but they were only making things worse. "Can we maybe not talk about it anymore?"

"Of course," Stella said with manufactured cheer. "Hey, did you guys see in the paper that the coffee shop is set to reopen next week? And construction on the hospital will begin next month. I'm not sure if it's possible, but I'd like to have the new city hall building completed by the first anniversary of the tornado. We've come so far already in our rebuilding efforts."

"It's definitely starting to look like home again," Lark said.

The rest of the meal was awkward to say the least. No one brought Amelia up again, but considering the occasional sideways glances and sympathetic smiles from her friends, the subject was clearly on everyone's mind.

It would have been easy for her to make some sort of excuse and leave the diner, but Julie forced herself to sit there and pick at her salad, pretending to follow the conversation, when inside she was all jumbled up. She wondered how much time he'd been spending with Amelia. He'd come home very late from the hospital the past two nights. Could he have been with Amelia? Had they rekindled their romance? Was it possible that he was sleeping with her?

The thought made Julie sick to her stomach, though it shouldn't have. They never said they wouldn't see other people. Julie had just assumed, in the spirit of making their marriage look legitimate, and because they were intimately involved, that they wouldn't. And though she wanted to put it out of her mind and let it go, her brain went into overdrive instead.

She picked at her food and sipped her sweet iced tea, when what she really needed was something big and alcoholic. Anything to loosen the knots in her chest, to sooth her bruised pride.

The lunch seemed to go on forever, but Julie refused to be the first one to leave.

Claiming she had more establishments to visit, Stella left first, and then Lark got a call from the hospital and had to rush back to work, leaving just Julie and Megan.

"Julie, I am so sorry," Megan said the instant they were alone. "We never meant to embarrass you that way. We just…"

"Assumed that as his wife Luc would have told me. I would have thought so, too."

"I'm sure he had a good reason for not saying anything. And I'm sure nothing is going on between them."

"Are you sure? Really? If nothing was going on, why would he hide it from me?" She heard herself and shook her head with disgust.

"As your friend, husband and boss, he should have had the courtesy to tell you. You have every right to be angry with him."

At this point Julie wasn't sure what she was feeling. Or what she *should* feel. If the tables were turned, would she have done anything differently?

Yes, she would have. She would have told him the truth. She wondered how she could be so blind to what had been going on around her. Had she just been lulled into a false sense of security? And why hadn't anyone told her?

"What exactly have you heard about her?" Julie asked Megan.

Megan hesitated. "Maybe you should talk to Luc about it."

Oh, she would, but first she wanted the entire story, or as much as Megan could tell her. "I want to know what you've heard. I thought she was married."

"Divorced."

Swell. "What else?"

Looking pained, Megan said, "I heard they've been spending a considerable amount of time together. But that could just be talk."

She doubted it. "How much longer will she be here?"

"I really don't know. Her son is having spinal surgery, so as long as it takes him to recover I guess."

At least a week, maybe a little longer. That wasn't too bad. "Did Luc do the surgery yet?"

Megan shook her head. "And I have no idea when he's supposed to do it. Soon, I would imagine."

Not soon enough as far as Julie was concerned. The faster they left, the better. Unless it was already too late. Maybe he'd fallen back in love with her. Which would mean what for Julie? Divorce? Deportation? Or would she simply have to share him until she became a legal citizen?

What a horrifying thought.

For the rest of the day Julie walked around with a knot in her chest. And though she had no right to, she felt angry and betrayed. She went back to the hospital and tried to work, but she couldn't concentrate worth a damn. What she wanted to do was confront Luc, but she was still too hot under the collar. She needed time to cool off and put things into perspective. Convince herself that technically, Luc had done nothing wrong.

She left work early and headed for home, wondering how much longer she would actually be calling this grand place home. Would Luc move Julie out, and bring Amelia and her son in? Or would they all live there together as one big happy family? The idea made her shudder.

She wandered the house aimlessly for several minutes, confused and scared, her thoughts too jumbled to be rational, wondering what her next move should be. Should she confront Luc, or let him tell her in his own good time? And what if she didn't like what he had to say?

She wound up in the den, with its ceiling-high stone fireplace and panoramic windows, staring blankly into the afternoon sunshine, feeling as if the perfect life she'd had just this morning had completely fallen apart.

"You're home early," she heard Elizabeth say, and turned to see her wheeling her chair into the room. "How's my favorite daughter-in-law today?"

She said it with a smile so filled with love and genuine affection, Julie burst into tears.

An emergency surgery came in just as Luc was about to leave the hospital, so by the time he finally did get home it was after eleven. He went straight to Julie's room to tell her about Amelia, but she was already asleep.

"Julie," he called softly, but he didn't get an answer. He considered waking her, but he figured the news would be much better received after they both had a good night's sleep.

His stomach rumbled, reminding him that he'd skipped dinner, so he went down to the kitchen for a snack. He foraged though the fridge and found a pot of leftover stew.

"You're home late," he heard his mother say, and turned to see her wheeling herself into the kitchen. She was in her pajamas, but clearly hadn't been to bed yet.

"What are you doing up?" he asked her. "You know how important it is that you get your rest."

"Where have you been?" she asked.

"The hospital."

"Doing what?"

He frowned. What did she think he would be doing? "I had an emergency surgery. Why? Is something wrong?"

"Come here," she said, gesturing him to her.

He set the pot on the stove and walked over to her.

"Down here," she said, and he leaned over, thinking she wanted to give him a hug. Instead she whacked him upside the head.

Hard.

"Ow! Jesus," he said, seeing stars, rubbing the pain away. He could say with confidence that her strength was definitely coming back. "What the hell was that for?"

"Amelia is here," she said, and her tone said she wasn't at all pleased about it.

"Yes. Her son is my patient."

"And you didn't think this was something your wife might have liked to know?"

Aw, hell. "I was going to tell her tonight when I got home. I take it she already knows?"

"Of course she knows! The way people talk around here, how long did you think you could keep it a secret?"

"I wasn't keeping it a secret." He just hadn't brought it up.

"And the way she found out…" She pressed her lips together in a thin line, shaking her head. "What were you thinking?"

"I honestly didn't think it was a big deal—"

"Not a big deal?" she shrieked, her eyes wide, and he backed up a step, just in case she took another swing at him.

"—until today," he finished. "Drew warned me that Amelia has been all around town making noise like she and I have some sort of relationship, but it's not true."

"That's a little hard to believe, all things considered," his mother said.

Did she actually believe the lies Amelia had been spreading? And if she did, had Julie believed them, as well?

"How did Julie find out?"

His mother explained that she'd been out with her friends when the subject came up, and that everyone knew but her. "The poor thing was beyond humiliated."

He cursed under his breath. He never meant for it to go this far. He should have known Amelia would do something like this. "I intended to tell her tonight."

"Well, you're too late. And you owe her an apology."

"Of course I'll apologize."

"Not only are you a lousy excuse for a husband, you're not a very good friend, either."

Damn, she really was furious. "You don't think that's a little harsh?"

"Not in the least. Honesty and trust are the basis for any relationship. Platonic or romantic. You lied to her."

Technically, he hadn't, but he knew what his mother would say, because he'd heard it a million times growing up. A lie by omission was still a lie. "As I said, I didn't think it was relevant. I had no idea Amelia was spreading rumors."

"The poor thing sobbed on my shoulder."

He blinked. "Amelia?"

"No, you idiot. Julie."

Julie *cried*?

Julie?

In all the years he'd known her, through the worst conditions and situations, he'd never so much as seen her well up. She had tenacity, and nerves of steel. She really must have been humiliated to get that upset. And he felt like a louse for putting her in that position. His mother was right. He was an idiot. And a sad excuse for a spouse. And an even worse friend. Had he honestly believed that by avoiding Amelia, she would have no impact on his life? Or Julie's? This was Amelia they were talking about; he should have known better.

"Are you still in love with her?" his mother asked.

"Julie?"

She rolled her eyes. *"Amelia."*

The fact that she would even ask that question was a clear indication of just how far out of hand this had gotten. In retrospect, all this time later, he wasn't sure if he'd ever loved her. If it had instead been a case of extreme infatuation. "I do not love her. I have no feelings for her whatsoever. I didn't intend for any of this to happen."

"But it did happen, and you need to fix it."

He intended to. First thing tomorrow he would talk to Julie.

Ten

After tossing and turning most of the night, Julie dragged herself out of bed at the crack of dawn, relieved to discover that Luc was still sleeping. She'd heard him come in last night, but feigned sleep when he opened her bedroom door. Late as he was, it didn't take a genius to know where he'd been. And whom he'd been with.

She knew they needed to talk about it, but she needed to get her head on straight first. It was weird how quickly things could change. One minute everything was fine and going as planned, the next she didn't have a clue what to expect. But it wasn't Luc's fault, or hers. Neither of them could have anticipated this happening. But if he wanted Amelia, Julie wouldn't stand in his way.

If Luc were to divorce her so soon after the wedding, the immigration people would be suspicious to say the least. She needed to formulate a plan, an exit strategy that wouldn't involve deportation though the idea of staying Royal had lost its appeal. It would be too humiliating. There was nothing for her in South Africa. Maybe she could move closer to her sister, find a new job.

She sat in her office at the hospital, staring blankly at her laptop, her mind moving in so many directions at once, she couldn't make sense of anything. And she dreaded the moment Luc walked through her office door wanting to talk, because she had no idea what to say to him, or how she was even supposed to feel.

Several minutes had passed when she heard a knock on her door. Her heart raced up to her throat and her knees went all soft and squishy.

Here we go.

She took a deep breath and looked up, expecting to see Luc, but when she saw who was really standing there, her heart plummeted to the pit of her stomach. She'd seen that face before, in a photo Luc used to carry in his wallet. For all she knew it was still in there.

Amelia looked so harmless, her skin pale, her hair flat and lifeless and in need of washing, Julie almost felt sorry for her. Having a child with a chronic illness had obviously taken its toll on her.

"Hi, there," she said, looking nervously around the office. She spoke with one of those adorable Southern accents, and despite looking a little run-down and tired, she was still a very beautiful woman.

"Hello, Amelia, I'm Julie."

"You know who I am?"

Unfortunately.

Julie rose from her chair and crossed to the door, reaching out to shake her hand. It was small and delicate, just like the rest of her, but her grip was firm.

"I hope I'm not interrupting anything," Amelia said. "I just had to meet the woman who finally got a ring on Luc's finger."

The way Julie understood it, Luc had been more

than ready to settle down with Amelia. It was she who ran off with someone else. Which obviously hadn't worked out very well for her.

"Have you got a minute?" Amelia asked her. "Can we talk?"

"Come in." As much as Julie wasn't looking forward to this, she knew that it would be best to clear the air. Since Luc didn't seem inclined to talk to her about it, she could hear it straight from the source. At least here, in her office, she had the upper hand. Amelia was in her territory.

Amelia stepped inside. Julie shut the door and gestured to the chair across her desk. "Sit down."

Amelia hesitated, looking conflicted. "Are you sure? I know this is awkward…"

Not as awkward as it would be if they didn't talk. "I'm sure. Please, sit."

Amelia sat on the very edge of the seat, as if she might jump up at any second and bolt for the door. Julie returned to her chair and sat.

"I understand there's been talk," Amelia said. "I wanted to clear the air. I'm not sure what Luc has told you…"

Not a single damned thing, but she didn't tell Amelia that. When in doubt, change the subject. "First, how is your son?"

At the mere mention of her boy, her face lit. "Antsy. Ready for his surgery, but still a little scared. He knows his recovery will be slow and painful. But he can't wait to get on his feet again so he can play with his friends. He's crazy about baseball, and for a five-year-old he's really good, too.

"The last few months, as he's become more and

more limited physically, have been very hard for Tommy. Tommy's father, my ex-husband, rarely sees him. He never could forgive me for giving birth to a less than perfect child."

"I'm sorry to hear that," Julie said, feeling sympathy for the boy. She knew too well what it was like to grow up in a single parent home. Though her father, at best, was never more than half a parent. *At best.*

"He traded me in for a younger model," Amelia said with a weak smile. "I guess that's what happens when you marry for money and social standing."

The admission surprised Julie, and it must have shown.

"I don't deny that I've made many mistakes," Amelia said, head held up proudly. "My only regret is how it's affected my son. After all he's been through, he deserves better. He deserves a father who gives more than a monthly check."

"He has you," Julie said. "What more could he possibly need?" She would have given anything to have her mother back, for her parents to trade places. For her father to be the one who died.

Tears welled in Amelia's eyes. "My gosh," she said, dabbing at them. "You are just so sweet. I want you to know that when I came here I had no idea that Luc was married. He's a lucky man."

"I'm the lucky one," she said, and it was true. It was a wonderful thing he was doing for her and she couldn't lose sight of that. Even if he did fall back in love with this adorable woman. Who would blame him?

"I hear a bit of an accent there," Amelia said, cocking her head slightly. "Where are you from?"

"South Africa. But my parents were from Wales originally."

"Were from? They're not with you anymore?"

"No."

"Mine are alive and kicking," Amelia said with a sigh of exasperation. "And still trying to tell me how to run my life."

"I'm sure they mean well."

"No, they're just nosy and controlling. They always have been. I swore that when my Tommy was born, I would allow him to grow up to be whatever he wants to be. Play with the friends he likes regardless of their social standing, marry the girl he loves even if she's penniless. All of the things I never had. I'll even let him go to public school if that's what he decides he wants."

It sounded as if she and Amanda had quite a bit in common when it came to family. "My sister and I went to a private girl's school," Julie told her. "I hated it. I never felt as if I fit in."

"And I fit in too well. I was an entitled, spoiled brat. If not for my Tommy, I probably still would be, but having him has taught me so much about what really matters, you know?"

Julie could only imagine.

Amelia relaxed back into her seat, looking a bit less as if she might bolt. "How did you and Luc meet?"

"We were both volunteering for Doctors Without Borders."

"Oh, you're a doctor, too?"

"No. Currently I'm Luc's research assistant."

"Research for what?"

"Luc's medical inventions and surgical techniques.

They've made him quite famous in the medical community." And very wealthy.

"What is it that you do exactly?" Amelia said, looking genuinely interested.

"I conduct interviews, collect data and statistics."

"So you must see him a lot."

"Actually, no. As chief of surgery for the hospital, he's always on call. There are days when I barely see him."

Amelia scrunched up her nose. "Don't you hate that?"

"That's just the way it is," she said. "The way it's always been. But I work long hours as well, so I can't really complain." Nor would she ever feel the need.

"I used to hate that Luc's career meant more to him than I did. I was so jealous. At the time, I was used to getting what I wanted, and he did try to accommodate me. Looking back now, I have to wonder why he stuck around as long as he had. Why he wasn't the one who dumped me. I was such a bitch sometimes."

Julie had no answer for her. But she was guessing it was because he loved her, and he was willing to overlook the not-so-perfect stuff.

"He's still mad at me," Amelia said, eyes lowered. "I feel so bad for the way I treated him and I was really hoping we could put the past to rest, but that doesn't seem very likely. He won't even talk to me."

"Just give him time. I'm sure he'll come around."

"I appreciate the encouragement, but I think it's misplaced. And you're probably the last person I should be confiding in about this. To be honest, I'm not even sure why you're talking to me. If the situation were reversed, I wouldn't talk to me. Or if I did, I would tell me to stay the hell away from my husband. Why aren't you, by the way?"

Because he isn't really my husband. "You two clearly have unresolved issues. It's in both your best interests to deal with them so you can move on."

"That's all I want."

Julie wasn't sure she believed that. She didn't not believe it, either. Luc had always described Amelia as cold, heartless and manipulative. To Julie, she just seemed sort of…pathetic.

"How is his mom doing? I heard that she's been sick. It must be difficult for him, as close as they are."

"It is."

"Do you get along with her?"

Julie hesitated and Amelia cringed.

"Am I getting too personal? I'm sorry if I am. I'm just curious. Too curious for my own good, my daddy used to claim."

"Yes, we get along. I consider her one of my closest friends."

"She hated me—but I didn't like her, either. She and Luc were very close and I was threatened by that."

Elizabeth was as down-to-earth and easygoing as her son. It was hard to imagine her *hating* anyone. And Julie had always considered his close relationship with his mother a good thing. She'd certainly never felt threatened or jealous.

Amelia must have read her mind. "I don't blame her for not liking me. I was different back then. I was very much into appearances. Her disability made me uncomfortable and I'm sure it showed. I'd never known anyone in a wheelchair. I had no idea how to act around her. I realize now how ridiculous it was for me to let her disability define who she was as a person. The idea of someone judging my Tommy based on his physical capacities makes my heart hurt. I feel as if I owe her an apology. I asked Luc if I could visit her. He didn't seem to think that was a good idea."

"Her health is compromised, leaving her vulnerable to infection. I'm sure that's the reason." Though to be honest, she really wasn't sure.

"And I'm sure that you're just saying that to make me feel better," Amelia said with a sad smile. "But I appreciate the effort. I guess some things just aren't fixable."

She genuinely seemed to want to rectify her past mistakes. Luc should at least give her the chance to explain, for both their sakes. "I'll talk to Luc and see what I can do, but no promises."

"You know," Amelia said, "you're not at all what I expected."

When Julie smiled, she really meant it. "Neither are you."

That morning, the instant he stepped through the hospital doors an hour later than usual, Luc was ambushed by half a dozen people needing him for one thing or another. Sign this. Initial that. Should it be the red or the blue pill? It was the major drawback of being chief of surgery. When he did finally get to his office, Ruth greeted him with one brow raised, looking from him to her watch, then back to him again. "Working a half day, are we?"

"I know, I was up late and slept through my alarm." All night, Luc had been attuned to even the slightest noise coming from Julie's room across the hall. When she woke he wanted to talk to her, but he never got the chance. The last time he looked at the clock it had been four forty-five and still dark. When he opened his eyes again, sunlight was pouring through the blinds and the clock said 7:38 a.m. He'd gotten up and checked Julie's room, but of course she was gone.

He took off his suit jacket and waited for Ruth to get up and retrieve his lab coat, but she just sat there. "Lab coat?" he said, expecting her to jump to attention.

She didn't.

"I'm very busy," she said, but she just sat there, arms crossed, glaring. She didn't look busy to him. She did look pissed off though.

"Did I do something to upset you?" he asked her.

"Like what?"

"I have no idea. That's why I'm asking."

"It wouldn't have anything to do with the fact that a week after your wedding you're hooking up with ex-girlfriends?"

"Hooking up?" He'd never heard her use the vernacular of a much younger generation. "Do you even know what that means?"

"I know that what you're doing is wrong," she said, chin tilted stubbornly. "How do you think this will make Julie feel?"

Pretty lousy if what his mom said was true. "Cancel anything I have before noon," he told Ruth, getting the lab coat himself. He had a lot of explaining to do, and he had the feeling it might take a while. "And for the record, I am not hooking up with Amelia. I've barely spoken to her."

"That's not what I've heard."

And he didn't have the time to sit there and explain. Ruth's feelings on the matter were the least of his worries.

He headed to Julie's office three floors up. He knocked on the door, hoping she was there.

"Come in," she called, so he opened the door…and got the shock of his life when he realized Amelia was sitting there with Julie.

Talk about awkward.

Or was it? Julie and Amelia looked completely at ease with each other.

"What the hell is this?" he asked, his tone sharper than he intended, feeling like the odd man out.

Julie looked at Amelia, and Amelia looked at her, and then both women burst out laughing.

Eleven

"We weren't laughing *at* you," Julie insisted to Luc several minutes later after Amelia left her office and they were alone.

"You looked right at me and laughed," he said, not sure who irritated him more, Julie or Amelia. Or maybe it was how cozy the two of them had looked sitting there together. This was not supposed to happen. Julie was supposed to dislike Amelia as much as he did.

"Not ten seconds before you knocked we were talking about how you would react if you walked in and saw us together," Julie said. "It's the timing that had us laughing. Not you."

It sure hadn't felt that way. He sat on the corner of her desk. "We need to talk."

"About what?"

About what? Was she joking? "For starters, what Amelia was doing here."

Julie shrugged. "We were talking."

Thanks, Captain Obvious. "I could see that. What were you talking about?"

"You, mostly."

Swell. Did he even want to know what was being said? Probably not.

"I should have told you that she was here," he said. "And that her son is my patient. And I know the fact I didn't looks suspicious—"

"*Luc*, stop. You don't owe me an explanation."

Of course he did. "We're married, I should have said something about her being here."

"This marriage is only pretend, remember?"

He was getting a little tired of her reminding him of that. Who was she trying to convince, him or herself? "Then, as your friend, I should have told you."

"I'm sure you had your reasons not to. Besides, I think it's good that you're finally getting a chance to settle things with her. You should have done it a long time ago."

"There's nothing to settle."

"For her there is."

"That's not my problem. And despite what you've probably heard, I have not been spending time with her. She, on the other hand, has been stalking me."

"I know. She told me."

He blinked. "She did?"

"Well, she didn't use the term *stalking*, but I know she's been trying to see you. All she wants to do is talk."

"You believe that?"

"Unless I hear otherwise from you, what reason do I have not to?"

He could think of a couple dozen. "You don't know her the way I do."

"People do change."

Not people like her. "She's the same old Amelia, trust me."

"How can you know that if you won't talk to her?"

He knew Amelia was manipulative, but to coax Julie over to her camp with a single conversation? That was quite an accomplishment, even for her. "As I said, I have no need or desire to discuss or settle anything from our past. Period."

"She's been through a lot. I really think that she's different now. Who knows, she may still be the love of your life."

Oh, good God no, she wasn't. "She is not the love of my life."

"Either way, it's okay with me if you spend some time getting to know her again. And if you decide you need to end our marriage—"

"Absolutely not." Was she serious? What kind of friend would he be? Besides, he would choose Julie over Amelia any day of the week. The trouble was making her believe that. Julie had never had a man in her life who hadn't disappointed her deeply in one way or another. It was almost as if she expected it, planned for it even. He refused to let that happen to her again. He wouldn't let her down, no matter what he had to do. "Until you get your permanent citizenship you're stuck with me. As long as it takes. I don't go back on my promises." He took her hand and squeezed it hard, his eyes locked on hers. "I mean that. I don't want this to come between us. You're the most important person in my life."

"It won't come between us."

"You promise?"

She smiled. A *real* smile. "I promise."

Somehow that just didn't seem good enough. There was something else going on here that he just couldn't seem to put his finger on. "Are you sure you're okay? My mom said you cried. You never cry."

Her cheeks blushed a vivid shade of pink. She never cried, and she blushed even less often. "I wish she wouldn't have said anything to you. It was really, really embarrassing."

"She was concerned."

"It was PMS, that's all. Every now and then it makes me emotional. And for the record, I do cry occasionally. I just don't let anyone else see it. It was just bad timing."

"So, if you have PMS, I guess that means you're not…"

"I'm not pregnant."

He waited for the relief to flow over him, but weirdly enough, he felt a twinge of disappointment instead. He wasn't ready to be a parent, and neither was Julie, but knowing there had been a slight possibility, it had gotten him thinking. But the timing couldn't have been worse. And he was completely overlooking the fact that, as she liked to point out, he and Julie were married in name only.

"I was thinking, if you're going to be seeing Amelia—"

"I'm *not*. I'm married to *you*, and until that changes I'm not *seeing* anyone else."

"I was just going to say, you should try to keep it on the down low."

Was she giving him permission to cheat on her? Did she really believe he would put her citizenship in jeopardy? Not to mention her dignity. And his own. And their *friendship*. What sort of man did she think he was? "It's not going to happen. Not now, not ever. I don't find her even remotely attractive."

"You can't deny that she's beautiful."

On the outside maybe. "As far as I'm concerned, she's nothing more than the mother of my patient. That's as far as it goes now, or ever will go. Amelia and I had our shot and she blew it. She doesn't get a second chance."

"I think she's really changed."

Somehow he doubted that. Amelia liked to manipulate, and she was good at it. He didn't doubt that she was manipulating Julie. Julie's instincts when judging a person's character had never been stellar, but she'd had Luc around a good majority of the past six years to give her guidance. She'd always listened to him before. Why not now? "Are you that eager to get rid of me?"

"Of course not," she said, laying her hand on his arm. Her skin was soft and warm. Whenever she touched him, something happened, something deep down inside of him shifted. He'd never been with a woman who could excite him the way she did, or frustrate him, while at the same time making him feel more at peace than he ever had in his life.

"I just want you to be happy," she said.

"Then, please trust me when I say to stay away from her. *That* will make me happy."

"Why?"

"She's not the person you think she is." Julie was too trusting, too nice to see Amelia for what she really was. Amelia would chew her up and spit her back out without batting an eyelash.

"We'll see," Julie told him, as if she knew something he didn't. Some significant piece to the puzzle that hadn't yet fallen into place.

Chumming up to him was one thing, but why would

Amelia befriend Julie? What did she possibly stand to gain? Or was she just screwing with his head, hoping to cause chaos? Anything to make herself the center of attention.

"What do you think of cats?" Julie asked, and the abrupt change of subject threw him for a second.

"I think they're delicious. Why?"

She laughed, and it was truly like music to his ears. He liked making her happy, seeing her smile.

"I'm being serious. Do you like them?"

"I don't *dis*like them. We had several at the ranch when I was growing up. But they were always more of my mother's thing."

She frowned. "Oh."

"Why do you ask?"

"The shelter is filled beyond capacity, and I've never actually had a pet, so I thought maybe a kitten…but it sounds like it would be a bad idea."

"Why not a dog? I like dogs."

"Let's be honest. Neither of us has the time for a dog. Our schedules are just too busy."

He couldn't deny that. "You're right. But a cat?" He made a sour face. "They're so…sneaky."

"Never mind. Like I said, it was just a thought."

She sure didn't put up much of a fight.

He shrugged apologetically and said, "Sorry."

"No, it's okay," she said, forcing a smile. And not a very convincing one. "I've gone this long without one. When I get my own place I'll have to find a pet-friendly apartment this time."

Though he knew it was inevitable, the thought of her eventually moving out didn't sit well with him. He liked having her there, knowing that she was just across the hall if he needed her, or if she needed him. Though he would much rather she be a permanent addition to his bed, even if all they intended to do was sleep. He'd gently suggested on more than one occasion that she stay the night in his room, but she never would. Their wedding night had been the only exception.

"I'm used to sleeping alone," she'd explained, but he had the feeling it was more than that. He just wasn't sure what. He'd begun to wonder if this friends with benefits deal they had going was a little more complicated than either had expected. Aside from the sex, their relationship hadn't changed, so why did everything feel so...different? Was he falling in love with her? For real? And if he was, what next? Did he take the chance and tell her? If she didn't share those feelings, he knew it would only drive her away.

That wasn't a risk he was willing to take.

Twelve

Julie believed Amelia when she said she only wanted to talk to Luc, but she seemed to be the only one in town who did.

"Everyone hates me," she told Julie that Friday, while they shared lunch in the hospital cafeteria. When Tommy slept, which was quite often due to the heavy dose of pain meds that he was on, Amelia would sometimes sneak away and visit Julie. She was the only friend Amelia had in town, and though they were an unlikely pair all things considered, they had quite a bit in common.

"I'm sure no one hates you," Julie said, though she, too, noticed Amelia getting the cold shoulder and more than a few suspicious looks. "Luc is a respected member of the community. People are just very protective of him."

"I noticed," Amelia said, moving her food around her plate, but not really eating much. With her son's surgery scheduled soon she was understandably edgy. "I'm getting sick of hospital food, so I went to the diner last night. But I got so many dirty looks I had to leave. Even the waitress gave me the cold shoulder. I had them wrap my food up and I took it back to the hospital to eat."

Julie hated that people would treat her that way when they didn't even know the full story. Didn't even know Amelia. Did no one care that she had a sick child? Why couldn't they cut her a little slack? "If they knew you like I do, they wouldn't act that way."

"They don't want to know me," she said. "I can see now that coming here was a mistake. After the surgery, as soon as Tommy is stable enough to be moved, I'm going back to Houston. I'm as big a joke there as I am here, but at least there I don't get sneered at every time I walk down the street. They're kind enough to do it behind my back. The poor little debutante with the sick kid whose husband couldn't keep it in his pants."

Julie cringed. "Ouch."

"I know. And my parents hold me personally responsible for tarnishing our family reputation."

That was just wrong, but Julie knew from experience how unreasonable parents could be. "How is your husband cheating on you your fault?"

"Oh, they didn't care about the cheating. That's just what husbands do, apparently."

"According to who?"

"Houston high society."

"That's crazy," Julie said.

"At first Tom, my ex, was very discreet, but I knew something was up. He'd work lots of late nights and went on weekend business trips. I fooled myself into thinking that I was imagining things. I was used to men fawning all over me. I was young and beautiful and rich, and I knew it. It was a blow to my pride to think that my husband, the man who was supposed to worship the ground I walked on, would stray.

"I was sure that fatherhood would settle him down."

"Did it?"

She shook her head. "It only seemed to push him further away. Tom was never there for our son, not even when he was an infant. Even less after he was diagnosed. All the money and status in the world wasn't worth my baby being treated that way."

"What did you do?"

"I got really, really angry. Then I said enough is enough and divorced him."

Julie admired any woman who had the courage to stand up for herself in the face of adversity.

"For what it's worth, I never would have had the guts to do what you did," Julie said.

"Humiliation is one hell of a motivator."

Julie told Amelia about her abusive ex, and how long it took her to screw up the courage to walk away. "He completely shredded my self-esteem. I was weak and pathetic."

"You were doing the best you could with the skills you learned growing up."

"That's just the thing. I never learned how to defend myself."

"That's my point. You were totally ill equipped to deal with the situation, but you still got away. You prevailed."

"Not as soon as I should have."

"Julie, I stayed for over *four* years."

"But you were married with a son. There was nothing keeping me from leaving. Nothing but my own cowardice."

"Don't be so hard on yourself," Amelia said. "You're one of the bravest people I know."

For a second Julie was sure that she was joking. Brave? *Her?* "How could you possibly think that?"

"Look at all the extraordinary things you've done. You've traveled all over the world helping people. You ventured off on your own and turned a terrible situation into something really good. That takes guts."

Julie had never really thought of it like that before. "I guess so."

"As crazy as my parents drive me, my mother especially, the idea of completely cutting them from my life is terrifying. I think about it all the time, but I could never actually do it. Despite everything, their opinion still matters to me. You don't seem to let anyone else's opinions color your judgment. If you did, you sure wouldn't be sitting here with me. The town pariah. I thought talking to Luc's friends and the people in town might give me some insight into how to relate to him. To make him listen to me. Maybe find some common ground. All I've managed to do is make a whole bunch of enemies."

"What those people think shouldn't matter to you. You know your intentions were good. That's all that's important."

A frown furrowed her brow. "I guess."

After lunch Julie went back to her office, feeling bad for Amelia. She believed it would be in Amelia's and Luc's best interest to talk, to settle the past so they could both move forward, but if Luc refused, there wasn't much Julie could do about it.

Or could she?

She wasn't duplicitous by nature, but if the situation called for it, and she truly believed it could benefit Luc, even she could be a little creative.

* * *

A few hours later Julie's phone rang and she was surprised to see Elizabeth's number on the screen. Her first thought was that it was her nurse and something was terribly wrong. And if she was calling Julie, Luc must have been unreachable. But when she answered it was Elizabeth's voice, and she sounded just fine.

"Something arrived for you today," she told Julie. "Can you get away from work? You should probably come home and open it."

It was an odd request, to say the least. "Who is it from?"

"I'm not sure, but I think it might be perishable."

It was probably something from her sister, who had finally called Julie to congratulate her on her "pseudowedding"—Jennifer's exact words. She'd probably sent chocolates or a fruit basket. "Can't you just stick it in the fridge for now?"

"It wouldn't fit."

"Can you open it for me and tell me what it is?"

"I wouldn't feel right opening someone else's package," she said. "You should come home."

Julie looked at the pile of transcripts from the interviews she'd conducted with spinal patients, and had been hoping to review that afternoon, but for whatever reason her coming home now was important to Elizabeth, and that was good enough for her. "Let me finish up what I'm doing, then I'll come home. Give me thirty minutes."

"See you soon!"

That was a little strange, but, okay. She finished what she'd been working on and headed home, surprised to find Luc's Beamer in the garage next to his mother's van. What was he doing home so early?

Julie let herself into the house, hung her keys on the rack next to the door and called, "I'm home."

"In here!" Elizabeth called back from the vicinity of the living room. When Julie got there, she saw Elizabeth in her chair, and Luc sitting close by on the sofa. He was dressed casually in jeans and a polo shirt, and next to him on the cushion was a brown cardboard box. It was around eighteen square inches and from what she could see, unmarked. The top wasn't sealed, either. Nor did it look like it ever had been. It would have been pretty easy for anyone to peek inside.

"You're home early," she said.

"I am," he agreed, wearing what she could only describe as a sly smile. "I had a few things to take care of this afternoon."

There was a weird vibe in the room. A feeling of expectation. She looked from him to his mother. "Is everything okay?"

"Fine," he said. So why were they looking at her that way? As if something was about to happen.

"So is that it?" she asked, nodding to the box.

"That's it," Elizabeth said. "Open it."

Julie eyed it warily. Was something going to explode or jump out at her? Was this some sort of gag gift? Because it sure didn't look as if had been shipped there.

"Come on," Luc said, sliding the box closer to himself to give her room to sit. If it were something volatile he probably wouldn't do that. Right? Of course, if he were the type of man to give his wife a box of some volatile substance, she wouldn't be married to him.

She sat gingerly on the edge of the cushion. He slid

the box to her, and feeling a little nervous still, she reached for the top. She tested the weight of it, and it was definitely too light to be a fruit basket. Bracing herself, she lifted the flaps, sure she was in for a shock. And boy, did she get one when she looked inside. Curled up in the bottom of the box, on a hospital baby blanket, lay a sleeping ball of fluffy, snow-white fur with an itty-bitty pink nose and black tipped ears.

"Oh my gosh, it's a kitten!" she said, but by their smiles, it was clear that they both knew exactly what was inside the box. "Did you do this?" she asked Luc.

"My mom and I went to the shelter today."

"But...you said—"

"Did you honestly think I wouldn't let you have a cat?" he asked.

Actually, she had. He'd said no, and in her world, no meant no. "But I thought you didn't like cats."

"I said I didn't dislike them. Would I rather have a dog, yes, but as you said, we don't have the time."

"It would probably be best if I watch him for you while you both work," Elizabeth said. "Until he gets bigger and knows his way around the house."

"He?" Julie said, lifting him gently from the box. He was so small and fragile looking. As she cuddled him in her palms, he blinked his little eyes open and looked right at her, making a soft mewling sound, as if he was saying hello.

"He is a very special kitten," Luc said. "One that no one else wanted."

Who in their right mind wouldn't want this adorable little ball of fluff? "Is there something wrong with him? Is he sick?"

"He's blind," Luc said. He moved the box out of the

way so he could scoot closer. "I guess it's common in white cats. There were a dozen or so other kittens available, but Megan said the little ones go fast. I knew you would want an animal who really needed a good home. We looked at the older cats first, then Megan told me about this little guy. The second I saw him I knew he was perfect."

"He is perfect," Julie said, rubbing her cheek against the softness of his fur, and he started to purr. A surprisingly loud purr to be coming out of something so small. "He's just so tiny and sweet. I love him."

"There's the added bonus of him not jumping up on things," Luc said, rubbing the kitten under the chin with his index finger. "Since he wouldn't know where to jump."

"He really can't see anything?"

"Megan said he won't respond to visual stimulation. Otherwise he's perfectly healthy. He'll need shots eventually, but that's about it."

"How old is he?"

"Eight weeks."

He was wide-awake now and fussing to get free, so she set him down on her lap, but he didn't stay there long. He sniffed around the sofa cushions for a few seconds, then leaned way over the edge, and before she could grab him, toppled over and landed on his back on the rug.

"Oh no!" she said, reaching for him, thinking he might be hurt, but he got up on his feet, shook it off and started sniffing around the coffee table leg. "Resilient little thing, isn't he?"

"What will you name him?" Elizabeth asked.

"I'm not sure. I'd like to get to know him a little better before I give him a name."

The nurse came in the room looking for Elizabeth. "I'm sorry to interrupt, but it's time for your PT."

"Already?" Elizabeth said with a sigh. To keep the circulation moving in her legs she had a daily physical therapy session. "It can wait a while."

Luc shot her a look. *"Mother."*

"Fine, fine, I'll go," she mumbled, wheeling her chair from the room.

"So you like him?" Luc asked, even though it was pretty darned obvious.

"He's adorable."

"His litter pan and food are in the utility room. I wasn't sure where you would want to keep them."

"In my room for now, I guess." She scooped the kitten up before he could get far, but he didn't want to be held and struggled to get free. She set him back on the floor and watched him sniff around. "This is the sweetest thing anyone has ever done for me."

"And I know just how you can thank me," he said his lips tipping up in a sly grin. She knew that look, and what it meant. And she was more than happy to oblige.

She leaned in and kissed him, and when he slid his hand behind her neck and under the root of her ponytail, cradling her head in his palm, she was toast. Luc knew just what to do to get her engine revving, and right now, her gas pedal was to the floor.

"Maybe we should take this upstairs," she said. "If you have time."

"I could be persuaded to take the rest of the day off. How about you?"

"I don't know, my boss is kind of a hard-ass."

Luc grinned. "I think he could make an exception just this— Ow!"

He winced in pain, and she looked down to see her sweet little kitten climbing his leg, nails out.

"Hey, you," she said, carefully extracting him from Luc's slacks, hoping that he hadn't ruined them. "Climbing up pant legs, not cool."

"Beth warned me that he can be very mischievous," Luc said. "She said that we have to keep a close eye on him until he's familiar with the layout of the house."

Considering how big the house was, that could take a while, and she could hardly imagine anything so small and sweet being mischievous. How much damage could one tiny kitten do?

It didn't take long to find out.

Thirteen

They took the kitten along up to Luc's bedroom, putting him on his blanket in his box on the floor by the bed. Luc had never been a cat person. As a kid he pretty much ignored the ones they had on the ranch. But he couldn't deny that this little guy was kinda cute.

When he first walked into the shelter he'd been overwhelmed by the volume of animals in need of homes, and picking one seemed a daunting task. He'd wandered the facility looking in cages. His mother had been no help at all. Had it been up to her they would have left the place with a couple dozen felines. It had been Megan who swayed him in the right direction.

He had been looking at the older cats, the ones who had been in the shelter the longest, when Megan suggested a kitten.

"I would think that kittens would be pretty easy to place," he'd said. "Julie would choose a cat no one else wants."

"I have just the thing," Megan had said, steering him to a cage in the kitten section. "Someone brought in a litter last week, and this little guy is the only one left."

The second he saw the little white fur ball he was

sure Julie would love him, and when Megan told him the kitten was blind, he knew it was fate.

Julie was so independent and capable, not to mention practical, it wasn't often that she let him do anything really nice for her. So when she asked him about getting a cat he lunged at the opportunity. Nothing meant more to him than making her happy.

And she seemed happy now. But they barely had a chance to get started in bed before the kitten climbed up the side to join them.

"Down you go," Luc said, scooping him up and setting him back in his box. "This is your bed."

They had just taken off their socks when he was up there with them again, so back in the box he went. And back up he climbed a few seconds later.

"This is not working," Luc said, dropping the kitten into his box again, this time not quite so gently. And back up he came like a spring, clawing his way up the comforter. "Do we have any packing tape?"

Julie shot him a look. "If you're thinking we're going to tape his box closed, think again."

Okay, bad idea. "We could lock him in the bathroom."

He got another look.

"Have you got a better idea?" Luc asked, putting the kitten on the floor this time. "Shoo. Go play."

When he didn't immediately spring back up, they both sat there waiting, watching the edge of the bed for his reappearance.

A minute or so passed and no kitty. "You think he got the hint?" Luc said.

"Seems that way," Julie said, then she looked behind them and started to laugh. "I take that back."

Luc turned to see that the kitten had come up the opposite side of the mattress this time and was sitting behind them. He yawned and licked his paws, content as could be.

Luc sighed and shook his head. "Ideas?"

"Let's wait a minute and see what he does. He's got to be tired from all the climbing."

They sat and watched while the kitten sniffed around the bed for several minutes, nearly toppling over the edge a few times. He made his way to the head of the bed, up onto Luc's pillow, where he curled up in a ball and promptly fell asleep.

"So now what?" Luc asked.

"It's a king-size mattress," Julie said. "There's room for everyone."

It was a little strange at first, making love with an audience, even if that audience was asleep, but eventually Luc forgot he was even there. They stayed on their side and the kitten stayed on his, while Julie "thanked" Luc.

Afterward, as they lay there together, Julie cuddled up against him, the kitten woke up, toddled over and joined them. He flopped down on his back, right on Luc's chest.

"This is the best gift anyone has ever given me," Julie said. She tickled the kitten's belly and he attacked her hand.

They played with the kitten for a while, and then Julie grabbed her phone from the bedside table to check the time.

"Are you getting hungry?" she asked Luc.

He eyed her warily. "When I said cats are delicious, I was kidding."

She laughed and gave him a playful nudge. "It's almost dinnertime. And it's Friday. We should do something."

"We still haven't had that romantic dinner out that I promised you. We could get dressed up and go somewhere nice, just the two of us."

"Or we could see if your mom would like to join us. We could go to the diner. And if she's feeling up to it afterward maybe we could take her to see a movie."

"Are you sure that's what you want?" he asked her.

"She's been stuck at home for almost two weeks now, and she's definitely well enough to leave the house. I would feel guilty going out and leaving her home alone."

Luc grinned and shook his head.

"Why are you looking at me like that?" she asked him.

"You're an extraordinary woman, Julie."

She blinked. "I am?"

He nodded.

"Why?"

"I offer to take you out to an expensive, candlelit dinner, and you would rather spend the evening with my mother."

"She's my friend. I want her to be happy. You know that it's only a matter of time before she gets another infection."

"I know," he said, his heart aching at the thought of losing her. "She's getting more and more fragile."

"So let's have fun with her while we still can."

"What are we going to do with him?" Luc nodded toward the kitten, who had curled up between them on the comforter and was sound asleep again.

"He can stay in here," she said. "As long as he has food and water and a litter pan he should be fine. And we keep the door closed. How much trouble could one tiny kitten get into?"

They had a nice dinner with Luc's mother, then took her to the theater to see the latest chick flick. Julie knew for a fact that Luc would have picked an action film any day of the week. Frankly, so would Julie, but his mother wanted to see a romantic comedy. It was after eleven when they finally got home.

"I'll help the nurse get her into bed," Luc told Julie. "You should probably go up and check on the fur ball."

She headed upstairs, opened the door to Luc's bedroom and switched on the light. "Here kitty, kitty. Mummy's home."

He wasn't on the bed sleeping, where she would have expected him to be, but then what did she know about having a cat? The most she'd ever had petwise was a caterpillar in a glass jar, until her father saw it there and flushed it down the toilet.

"Kitty, kitty," she called, checking all around the bedroom and the bathroom. "Come to Mummy."

She waited, but when he didn't come trotting out to greet her she frowned. "Where are you, you silly kitten?"

There was no sign of him so she got on all fours to look under the bed. From behind her she heard, "I don't know what you're doing, but I like the view."

She turned to see Luc standing behind her. "I can't find the kitten."

"He's got to be here somewhere," he said. "Did you try the closet?"

"Not yet."

Luc headed that way while Julie crawled over to check under the chest of drawers.

"Um, Julie? I found him."

"Oh thank goodness." She jumped up and darted to his closet door to join Luc. She looked inside and gasped. It was as if a hurricane had torn through. A dozen or so of Luc's clean, pressed dress shirts lay in piles all over the floor like an Egyptian cotton rainbow, while several others hung half on and half off the hanger. From the cuff of one, dangling a good two feet from the floor, hung the kitten, his claw snagged.

"Oh my gosh!" Julie dashed to his rescue, carefully unsnagging his nails and cuddling him to her chest. "You poor baby. How long were you hanging there?"

Luc just looked around, shaking his head. "What was that you asked? 'How much trouble could one tiny kitten get into?'" He spread his arms wide. "Here's your answer."

"He has been busy, hasn't he? On the bright side he'll probably sleep well tonight."

"So I guess I should have listened to Megan when she said that he's mischievous."

"I'm sorry. I hope he didn't ruin them."

"You'll make it up to me," Luc said, and she didn't have to ask what he meant. She helped him clean up the kitten's mess, then spent the next hour or so making it up to him, and what a hardship that turned out to be.

After making love again, he asked her to stay with him all night. She said no, he said please. She couldn't recall him using the word *please* any of the previous times he'd asked her and hearing the word spoken so earnestly, seeing the earnest look in his eyes…well, she just couldn't tell him no.

"Just this once," she said, settling back against the pillows. "But I'm used to sleeping alone, so I'll probably toss and turn most of the night. I apologize in advance if I keep you awake."

"It's a king-size bed, you won't even know I'm over here," he said, but nothing could be further from the truth. He never even made it onto his own side. He curled up behind her, his arm draped across her hip. And as if that wasn't crowded enough, the kitten, who was clearly exhausted after his adventure, curled up on the pillow above her head. She was annoyed, and utterly content at the same time. She closed her eyes, mentally preparing herself for a long restless night, and when she opened them again, it was morning. Not only had she not had a lousy night's sleep, she felt well rested and full of energy.

Luc was gone, but he'd left a note on the pillow. "Volunteering at the clinic until noon. How about lunch in the hospital cafeteria at 1:00?"

She looked at the clock, stunned to find that it was almost 10:30 a.m. She grabbed her phone off the bedside table and typed up a quick text.

Lunch sounds great, see you at 1:00.

He responded a few seconds later with a happy face icon.

She would have plenty of time to shower and make a trip to the pet supply store.

Speaking of pets…

She reached up over her head to pet the kitten only

to realize that he was gone. *Here we go again*, she thought. She pushed herself up out of bed and threw on the T-shirt and panties she'd been wearing the night before. She looked in the obvious places first. Under the bed, in the closet by his food dish, in the bathroom by his litter. But she couldn't find him anywhere. Had he snuck out when Luc left?

She checked everywhere, every corner and nook. She even checked under the covers, in case he'd been sleeping beside her when she flipped the blanket off.

Nothing. It was as if he'd vanished.

Where the hell could he have gone? she wondered, a feeling of panic building in her chest. How in the world would she find him? In a house this huge it could take days.

She was checking behind the curtains one last time, and was about to initiate a whole house search, when she heard a loud and very unhappy-sounding meow. But it seemed to be coming from above her head. She looked up to find the kitten clinging to the curtain valance on top of the rod, and now that she took a better look at the curtain panel, she could see teeny tiny holes where his claws had sunk in. The little imp had climbed all the way up, and apparently couldn't find his way back down. "You are mischievous," she said, getting up on her tiptoes to scoop him up. "Let's not go up here again."

She put the kitten in his box, grabbed the rest of her things and walked across the hall to her own room.

She set the box on the bed. "You stay here while I take a shower."

She didn't really expect him to obey, so it was no surprise when he escaped the box, tumbled down from the mattress onto the floor, got back on his feet and followed her into the bathroom where he started digging around in his litter. He may have been blind, but he had no trouble getting around.

Figuring he would be safe in there with her, she shut the bathroom door, locking him in. She undressed, turned on the water and stepped into the shower, leaving the door open an inch, so she could hear him if he got into trouble again. Though she wasn't sure what kind of trouble he could get into. There was really nothing for him to climb. The room was all tile and porcelain, which he couldn't get his claws into.

She was lathering her hair when she saw the shower door move, and looked down to see the kitten poking his head in. "You don't want to come in here," she said, but that was exactly what he wanted. He took a tentative step inside, and when the outer edge of the spray hit his fur, he stopped, looking confused. She thought for sure that he would turn tail and run; instead, he walked right under the spray, rubbing against her ankle with his soaked white fur, crossed to the opposite side, then sat down and started to clean himself.

What the heck? A cat who liked water?

She picked him up and set him on the bath mat, but before she could get the door closed, he was back in the shower. After one more failed attempt she managed to get him out of the shower and the door closed.

She finished, toweled them both off—which he didn't seem to appreciate much—then blow-dried her hair and got dressed. By the time she was finished, the cat had pulled another vanishing act. It took another few minutes of searching and this time she found him playing inside a canvas bag on her closet floor.

She carried him down to the kitchen where Elizabeth was sitting having her morning coffee and reading the newspaper. "Oh, there's the little guy!" she said, and Julie set the still-damp ball of fur in her lap.

"What happened to him?" Elizabeth asked, frowning up at Julie. "He's all wet."

"He took a shower with me."

Elizabeth's brows rose in disbelief. "Cat's don't like water."

"Someone forgot to tell him that."

Looking perplexed, she said, "That's odd."

Julie shrugged. "Maybe it has something to do with him being blind. Or maybe he's just weird."

"How was his first night home?"

Julie grappled for the right word. "It was…eventful."

She told Elizabeth about Luc's shirts, the curtain incident and finding him in her closet.

"He was probably bored," Elizabeth said. "Kittens need lots of stimulation."

"I'm going this morning to buy him some toys."

Looking excited, Elizabeth asked, "Would you like me to watch him for you while you're gone?"

"You don't mind?"

"Of course not. Take all the time you need."

"I do have several errands I'd like to run." He looked pretty harmless sitting there in Elizabeth's lap licking the water from his fur, but Julie knew what a little terror he could be. "But are you sure? He's a handful."

"I've had lots of cats. I'm sure I can handle it."

Julie hoped so. Shy of locking him in her room alone for the day, which seemed cruel, she really had no other choice. At least until he was bigger.

"Can we talk for a minute?" she asked Elizabeth, taking a seat at the kitchen table.

"Of course, honey. You can talk to me about anything, you know that."

She did, but this was different. "I need a favor. And it's a big one."

"As long as it doesn't involve me getting up and dancing," she joked. "Name it."

"Luc mentioned that you'll be at the hospital Monday for an iron infusion."

"That's right."

"Would you come to Amelia's son's room while you're there. Just for a few minutes."

She sighed. "Julie, I know you and she have become friends, and against my better judgment I've kept my opinions to myself, but—"

"I know you two didn't get along, and I know how Luc feels about her, but she really has changed. She knows she treated you badly and she'd only like the chance to apologize. She's been carrying around a lot of guilt—"

"Which was her own doing," Elizabeth said sharply.

"She doesn't deny that."

"Luc may be a grown man, but he'll always be my baby, and she hurt him deeply."

"She wants to make amends."

"Did she ask you to ask me?"

"No. But she's my friend and I want to help her. She asked Luc if she could visit you but he wouldn't allow it."

Up went Elizabeth's hackles, and in a cutting tone she said, "Who I do and don't see is not his choice."

Julie knew Elizabeth would feel that way, which is

why she'd brought it up. If she was going to persuade Luc to talk to Amelia, she would need Elizabeth on her team. Was it a little underhanded and sneaky? Maybe so, but Julie believed deep in her heart that Luc needed to settle things with Amelia, and this was the only way she could see to make that happen.

"If I didn't know better, I might think that you were trying to push the two of them together," Elizabeth said.

"If they're meant to be together, nothing I do or don't do will change that."

"That's very convenient for you."

Julie blinked. "What is that supposed to mean?"

"It's the perfect excuse to keep him at arm's length."

"It's not that," Julie said, though Elizabeth's words hit a little too close to home. "Whether he falls in love with Amelia, or some other woman, I just want him to be happy."

"Have you considered the possibility that Luc might be in love with *you*?"

She considered and dismissed it. But not to protect herself as Elizabeth implied. Julie was a realist. She knew that sex did not always equal love. Not the forever kind.

"I really feel that he needs this to move forward," Julie told the older woman. "With me or anyone else."

Elizabeth sighed. "I suppose you're right."

"So...you'll talk to her?" Julie said.

"I'll think about it," Elizabeth said. "But no promises."

That was all Julie could ask. "Thank you."

"I wouldn't do this for just anybody."

"I know."

"Even though you and Luc are married in name only, I think of you as my daughter."

"And I consider you one of my closest friends." Elizabeth smiled.

"Well, I should get going. I'd like to stop by the hospital and check on Amelia. Her son's surgery is Tuesday and she's getting nervous."

"You really do like her," Elizabeth said, looking perplexed. "And you trust her?"

"I do. She just wants to make amends."

The older woman nodded slowly and said, "I'll keep that in mind."

Fourteen

Having never had an animal before, there had never been a need to patronize a pet supply store. The sheer volume of available products was mind-boggling. Julie stood in the cat food aisle for a good forty-five minutes reading labels and looking up online reviews on her phone. The litter aisle was a nightmare as well, and the toy aisle even worse. There were a bazillion choices of every shape and size. How was she supposed to know what a blind kitten would like to play with? Even something as simple as picking out a collar took forever.

She made her selections to the best of her ability, nearly having a stroke when the cashier rang it all up and gave her the total. No wonder the shelter was always desperate for donations. Everything was so expensive.

With the kitten taken care of, Julie drove to the hospital. She had a few spare minutes, so when she got there, she made a quick detour to Tommy's room. Amelia sat in a chair next to her son's bed reading to him. She smiled brightly when she saw Julie, but the dark smudges under her eyes said it had probably been a long night.

She patted her son's arm. "Wake up baby, look who's come to visit."

With effort, Tommy opened his eyes, flashed her a sleepy smile and said, "Hi, Julie," so softly she had to strain to hear him.

"How are you feeling today," she asked him, but he had already fallen back to sleep.

"They had to up his pain meds again," Amelia said, concern darkening her features as she gazed down at her son. "Thank God the surgery is Tuesday. I never thought I would hear myself say this, but I'm actually a little homesick."

"Understandable considering the way people have been treating you."

"It's lonely. Tommy sleeps most of the time, and no one else around here talks to me unless they have to."

Not only did she look exhausted, but she'd lost weight, meaning she probably wasn't eating properly. The last time they had lunch she'd only picked at her food. "Have you been sleeping?"

"As much as I can. The nurses come in at all hours of the night to check on Tommy and I'm a light sleeper, so they inevitably wake me up. I'm only able to catch an hour or two here and there. I could swear that sometimes they do it just to mess with me."

"You need some uninterrupted sleep," Julie told her. "In a *real* bed."

"I can't leave the hospital. I don't want Tommy to wake up alone."

"You're no good to Tommy if you don't take care of yourself."

Her expression said that she knew Julie was right.

"Are you working today?" Amelia asked her.

"Nope, I'm meeting Luc for lunch."

"Speak of the devil," Amelia said, looking past her to the door. Julie turned to find Luc entering the room.

"Am I late?" she asked with a smile, but he didn't smile back. Now what?

"I have the results of the blood test from this morning," he told Amelia in his "doctor" tone, and the grim look he wore made Julie's heart drop.

Amelia must have sensed that something was amiss, that it wasn't just Luc being his usual bitter self, because her face paled a shade and she asked, "Is something wrong?"

"Tommy's white count is up," he said.

"What does that mean?"

"It could mean that he has an infection somewhere."

"Which means what exactly?" Amelia asked him, and Julie could see that she was struggling to hold it together, to be strong for her son.

There was genuine compassion in Luc's tone when he said, "If it remains elevated we may have to postpone the surgery."

The devastation on Amelia's face made Julie's heart hurt for her. "How long?" she asked.

"It's hard to say until we know what we're dealing with. Days, a week. Maybe longer."

Amelia looked so pale and distraught Julie worried she might lose consciousness. Julie wasn't a hugger by nature, but she felt compelled to do something to ease her pain, and Amelia readily accepted her embrace.

"I'm so sorry," Julie said. "I know this is frustrating, but I'm sure he'll be better in no time."

Amelia clung to her for several seconds, then let go and blinked away the tears that hovered just inside her eyelids. She took a deep breath, pulled herself up by her bootstraps, lifted her chin and asked Luc, "What's our next move?"

"I'm going to start him on a round of broad spectrum antibiotics, and do more tests. See if we can pinpoint the problem."

"You think that will take care of it?"

He hesitated, then said, "I'm cautiously optimistic. But if you would like to get a second opinion—"

"No," she said firmly, shaking her head. "If I didn't trust your judgment we wouldn't be here. Do what you think is best."

A look passed between Luc and Amelia, and they both smiled. Was he finally coming around?

Julie felt as if a weight had been lifted from her shoulders. For a few seconds anyway, before she felt a sudden and intense twinge of something unpleasant.

It was envy, she realized. She *wanted* the two of them to bury the hatchet, so why would she feel jealous?

Jules, you're being ridiculous.

She shoved the feeling deep down where it belonged.

"I'll stop by later this afternoon to check on Tommy," Luc told Amelia, and she flashed him a grateful, if not exhausted smile.

Amelia needed sleep. Badly.

"Can I see you alone for a minute?" Julie asked Luc, nodding toward the door, and he followed her into the hall. "Let's go down by the nurses' station."

When they were far enough away that Amelia wouldn't hear them, Julie turned to him. "In light of what just happened in there, I have a favor to ask."

He looked confused. "Something happened?"

"You and Amelia had a moment."

"We did? When?"

"Just a minute ago. You smiled at each other."

"I smile at a lot of people."

Now he was just being difficult. "There was a connection. Don't deny it."

He shrugged and said, "If you say so."

Did he seriously not see it?

"You mentioned a favor," he said, wiggling his brows at her. "Your office or mine?"

She couldn't help but laugh. "Not that kind of favor. I was hoping you could maybe say something to the nurses about the way they've been treating Amelia. I would, but I feel as if it's not my place to tell them how to do their jobs. But if you say something—"

"I'll talk to everyone," he said.

One less thing to worry about. "Thank you."

"We should get down to the cafeteria," Luc said.

"About lunch…" She looked from her watch to Tommy's room.

"Go," he said with a grin. "Amelia needs you. We'll have lunch another day."

"You're sure? Thanks for understanding."

He reached up and touched her cheek. "I hope Amelia realizes how lucky she is to have you as a friend."

Julie knew that she did. "How late are you working?"

Luc looked at his watch. "I should be home for dinner."

She pushed up on her toes to kiss him goodbye, aiming for his cheek, but Luc had other ideas. He cupped the back of her head and pulled her close, slanting his mouth over hers, and then kissed her in clear view of everyone at the nurses' station. And not a hospital hallway sort of kiss. This was a bona fide, just-wait-until-I get-you-home kiss.

Public displays of affection usually made her uncomfortable, but she could feel herself melting against him as he drew her closer. Until someone at the nurses' station wolf-whistled.

She pulled away and grinned up at him, her cheeks warm and her blood pumping. "That was nice. A little inappropriate considering where we are, but still nice."

"You're my wife. I can kiss you however and wherever I want."

"Is that how it works?"

"Damn straight." His eyes locked on hers, and the look he gave her was so supercharged with desire her heart skipped a beat. He was playing a role, that's all. They both were. But something in his eyes said he may have forgotten that.

"But I'm not really your wife," she reminded him.

He took her hand, grazing his thumb over her wedding band. "As long as this ring is on your finger, you're my wife. In every sense of the word."

He looked so serious, as if he really meant it, which was as confusing as it was terrifying. And yes, maybe a little exciting, too. Not to mention totally unrealistic. "Aren't we a little far into the game to be changing the rules."

"Maybe I don't like the rules anymore."

Her heart jerked violently, and then raced ahead double time. What the heck was he trying to say? Did this have something to do with her decision to sleep in his bed last night? Was she unknowingly leading him on? That had certainly never been her intention.

She took a step back and he let go of her hand. "I'd better go."

"Eventually we'll have to talk about this."

No they wouldn't, because they had already talked about it. It was a done deal. His friendship meant too much to her to risk losing over a misguided sexual relationship. Even if it was really fantastic sex. "I'll see you later."

Looking resigned, he said, "See you later."

She could feel his eyes boring into her back as she walked to Amelia's room, but she was too chicken to turn around and face him. She was terrified of what she might see. Maybe it would be wise to put a little distance between them. Perhaps Luc was becoming a little too comfortable with the physical aspect of their relationship.

Amelia stood next to her son's window, gazing blindly out the window, looking distraught.

"Everything will be okay," Julie said.

Amelia turned to her. "Deep down, I know that."

Amelia would feel so much better if she could get some uninterrupted sleep, and was able to take a long hot shower. Or better yet, soak in a hot bath with essence of lavender and lots of bubbles. Which Julie just so happened to have at her condo...

Before she could talk herself out of it, Julie pulled her key ring out and unhooked the key for her condo. She crossed the room and handed it to a confused Amelia.

"What is this for?" she asked Julie.

"My condo. I want you to use it as a home base while you're here in Royal."

She looked warily at her sleeping son. "You know

how I feel about leaving the hospital. What if Tommy wakes up…"

"He'll be fine. The nurses will take good care of him."

Amelia looked from her son to Julie, and back again. "I don't know…"

"Have you seen yourself in a mirror lately? You look terrible."

Amelia sighed, her shoulders sagging. "And I feel terrible. But he needs me here."

"Does he need you, or is it that *you* need *him*?"

Amelia frowned.

"Do you think Tommy doesn't notice how you look? He needs you to be strong for him. You can't do that if you're about to collapse."

Julie's words clearly hit home. "I guess I could sneak out for a little while."

Feeling relieved, Julie jotted down the address for Amelia, who typed it into the GPS on her smart phone.

"You know, you're going to be a great mom some-day," Amelia told her.

It was meant as a compliment, but it made Julie's heart hurt. She wouldn't be a good mother, because she would never have children. If she couldn't set aside her fears and let her guard down for Luc, her best friend, there was little hope left of her ever finding Mr. Right.

Fifteen

Late that afternoon, when Luc pulled into the garage, Julie's car was gone. He felt both disappointed and relieved at the same time. They needed to talk, to figure this marriage out. Despite his best efforts to adhere to their "plan," to think with his head, his heart seemed to be calling the shots now. He wanted Julie, in every way a man could want a woman. But her unwillingness to even consider discussing it didn't bode well for him. And she was so insistent that he and Amelia settle their past, he couldn't help but feel that she was hoping that he and Amelia would fall back in love. That would certainly save Julie the task of confronting her feelings. The difficult ones, that she kept buried deep. Her heart was like a fortress, and he wasn't quite sure how he would tear the walls down.

Or if that was even possible.

Luc let himself into the house, and found his mother in the family room, by the window overlooking the garden, reading a book. On her lap, curled in a ball, slept the kitten.

"Babysitting?" he asked her with a grin. He'd suspected she would enjoy the kitten as much as Julie did.

"Houdini," his mother said, and in answer to his confused look, added, "That's the kitten's name."

"Why Houdini?"

"He's an escape artist, and once he gets away, finding him is almost impossible."

"He's white, how could you miss him?"

"You'll see. And when you're searching for him, do yourself a favor and look up. That's where he prefers to be."

"Up where?"

"Anywhere he can reach. If he can get his nails into it, he starts climbing and doesn't stop until he reaches the top."

"Like what?"

"A bed, curtains, a pant leg. A *bare* leg—and you can bet that my nurse wasn't happy about that. It doesn't matter as long as it takes him vertical."

Luc frowned. "He's blind. That could be very dangerous."

"I tried to explain that to him, but you know cats," she said with an exaggerated shrug, "they never listen to reason."

He shot her a look.

She smiled. "On the bright side he has a very hard head."

"And how do you know that?"

"Every now and then he gets overexcited, takes off running and slams headfirst into something. Usually a wall or a piece of furniture. I won't lie, it's hard not to laugh, but he just shakes it off and keeps going. Then, bam, he hits something else. He'll do that three or four times in one spot, until he learns the landscape. I think he's mapping out the house."

"With his head?"

His mother shrugged. "Whatever works, I guess."

Luc wondered if cats were capable of using that sort of logic. "I don't suppose you know where Julie is."

"She's sitting with Tommy while Amelia naps, so he won't wake up alone."

"Where is Amelia?"

"At Julie's condo. She insisted that Amelia go there and take a nap."

Julie's condo? Hadn't she given it up when she moved in with him? She'd never actually said she would, but he'd just assumed...

He sighed and shook his head. Wrong again.

"Dinner will be ready at seven," his mother told him, in a tone that said being late was unacceptable.

Which gave him just enough time for a couple of beers at the Texas Cattleman's Club.

He turned to leave, but she stopped him. "There's something I wanted to ask you."

"About what?"

"I'm having my blood transfusion tomorrow and Julie asked me to stop in and see Amelia while I'm there. She said Amelia wants to apologize to me."

"Will you let her?"

"That's what I'm not sure about. I feel as if forgiving her would mean being disloyal to you."

A week ago, he may have thought so, too. But this wasn't about him anymore. He was finally at peace with their past. Didn't Amelia deserve the same?

"You should talk to her," he said. "I didn't want to believe it either, but she really has changed."

His mother gasped softly. "Don't tell me you still have feelings for her."

The idea made him chuckle, because other than sympathy for her and her son, he didn't feel much of anything for her. "Not at all. And I wouldn't consider your speaking to her as disloyal. In fact, I think it would be good for both of you."

"She broke your heart."

"Only because I let her." And now it looked as if he might be in a similar situation with Julie. Would he chase her down, only to have her break his heart? He'd been patient these past weeks, but his patience was wearing very thin. Either she loved him or she didn't. He needed to know if they had a future together.

When he got to the club he took a seat at the bar, ordered a beer and settled in to watch the basketball game playing on the television. He'd had three beers when his phone rang. It was Julie. But he had no idea what to say to her.

He ignored the call, turned the ringer off on his phone and ordered a scotch

The bartender, who knew he normally didn't have more than a beer or two, regarded him with growing concern. "Everything okay?" he asked.

"I should think that's pretty obvious," Luc said, swirling the scotch in his glass. Then he drained it in one swallow, set the glass down a little too forcefully and tapped the bar for another.

"Not until you hand them over," the bartender said, holding out his hand.

Without argument Luc dug his keys out of his pocket and dropped them in his hand. He was no stranger to the end result of drinking and driving. He'd seen it far too many times to make the same mistake himself. If he had to he would walk home.

Everything was getting a bit fuzzy, so Luc wasn't sure how long he'd been sitting there or how many drinks he'd consumed when Drew sat down at the bar beside him.

"Hey," Drew said, gesturing to the bartender for a beer.

"Hey," Luc replied.

Drew took a long pull on his beer when it arrived, then set it down on the bar and asked Luc, "You want to talk about it?"

"About what?"

"Whichever sorrows you're drowning with that scotch."

Trying to drown, and failing miserably. In fact, Luc felt even worse than he had when he walked in the door.

"You gonna make me guess?" Drew asked.

"I'm in love with Julie." He'd never said that out loud before, and hearing those words come out of his own mouth was a little surreal. So he said it again. "I am in love with Julie."

"Are you trying to convince me or yourself?"

He laughed bitterly. "Drew, I would give anything to go back to way things were before, when I didn't know what I was missing. When being her best friend was enough. But being with her has changed me, and now I can't change back."

"What makes you think you have to?"

"She doesn't love me."

"I don't believe that for a second."

"Okay, she isn't *in love* with me."

"Have you told her that you're in love with her?"

"She won't give me the chance. I tried to talk to her about it today and she refused to listen. She wants things to stay just the way they are now. I'm worried that if I push her too hard, it will only drive her away." He used to believe that he could think his way out of any situation but this one had him stumped.

"So what are you going to do?"

"If I knew that, I wouldn't be sitting here. Maybe I shouldn't do anything yet. Maybe I should give her more time. Just keep doing what we've been doing. Everything was perfect until I brought it up today."

"It seems to me that if things were perfect, you wouldn't have had to bring it up."

He'd be damned if Drew wasn't spot on. As close as Luc and Julie were, emotionally and physically, he wanted more. Being Julie's friend just wasn't enough now. But was he willing to risk their friendship?

Maybe he didn't have a choice.

Looking thoughtful, Drew said, "Maybe what you need to do is shake her tree a little, see what falls out."

"I'm not sure what you mean."

"Nudge her out of her comfort zone. See what she does."

"And how would I do that?"

He shrugged. "She's your wife. You know her better than anyone. You'll think of something."

Luc thought he knew her. Now he wasn't so sure. Maybe all this time he'd only been letting her see what she wanted him to see.

Maybe deep down he didn't know her at all.

Sixteen

Sunday was supposed to be Julie and Luc's special day, but he spent the majority of it in bed nursing a hangover. They had planned to have breakfast at the diner, then check out the recently reopened organic produce store to buy fresh flowers. After their food settled they would take a long walk in the park. Then maybe they would head back home for some afternoon "exercise." Later he would take her to dinner, then it was back home to make love again.

Instead Luc spent Sunday in bed nursing a hangover. It didn't take a genius to know why Luc had gone out and gotten hammered.

She knew that sleeping in his bed had been a bad idea. She should have listened to her instincts. She'd given him the wrong impression, led him on. She'd made him fool himself into believing that he was in love with her. But men confused sex with love all of the time, right? Or was it the other way around?

Either way, she would be sleeping in her own bed from now on.

She and Luc barely said two words to each other all day. She slept in her own bed that night, though she didn't do all that much sleeping. Luc didn't even try to talk her into staying with him, and when she kissed him good-night his lips felt so cold. So passionless. She knew that in a day or two he would realize what a huge mistake he'd almost made thinking they should take their relationship to the next level. He would realize that they were better off as just friends, then everything would go back to normal. Everything would be okay.

The kind of baggage Julie carried around wasn't so easily shed. And the idea of opening those bags and rooting through the traumatic events of her childhood made her feel sick to her stomach.

Monday dragged by, and every time Julie tried to see or call Luc he was too busy to be disturbed. He was still upset. She got that, but he was going to have to let it go at some point, so they could get back to being best friends. One day of the silent treatment had taken its toll. She missed him. She just wanted things to go back to the way they used to be. Friends with benefits. Hell, if it meant restoring their friendship to its previous, uncomplicated manifestation, she would even be willing to end their physical relationship. Though that would seriously suck.

Tonight, she decided. After dinner she would take him aside and offer to have that talk he wanted. Now that he'd had a few days to think it over, she was positive he would agree that it was best for both of them if they just kept going the way they had been.

The only bright spot of the day was when she stopped in Tommy's room to find Amelia next to her sleeping son's bed, tears in her eyes.

Julie's heart sank. Was his infection worse? Would they be postponing the surgery? "What happened?"

Amelia turned to her and smiled. "His white count is back to normal. They're going ahead with the surgery tomorrow morning at seven a.m.!"

Julie was thrilled for Amelia and Tommy, but her happiness deflated like a balloon when she realized what that meant for her and Luc. With such a delicate surgery on his schedule, the last thing Luc needed was to be distracted by their marital issues. That conversation they were supposed to have would have to wait.

The day of Tommy's surgery, Julie left Houdini in Elizabeth's capable hands and drove to the hospital early, intending to spend her morning waiting with Amelia in her son's room.

She'd heard Luc getting ready for work, but stayed in her room until after he left. She didn't want to risk a confrontation on this very important morning. Besides, after having two whole days to think about it, he would come around. She knew he would. He just needed time to realize the mistake he'd made letting his heart overrule his head. Then they could go back to being best friends.

Julie stopped in the cafeteria for coffee and doughnuts on the way up, and by the time she got to Tommy's room they had already wheeled him out for surgery. Amelia was sitting cross-legged on her air mattress, looking surprisingly well-rested and calm.

Julie handed her one of the coffees and offered her a doughnut. "I figured you could use this. One cream, two sugars, right?"

"You're a goddess," Amelia said, taking them from her. "How are things going?"

Julie sat in the visitors chair by the window. "Good."

"Luc came in to see me a little while ago," Amelia told her, and at the mere mention of his name Julie's heart dropped. It had been doing that a lot—pretty much every time she thought of him or heard someone say his name. "He explained what will happen during the surgery, and what to expect when Tommy is out of recovery," Amelia was saying, and Julie struggled to stay focused, but all she could think about was her looming conversation with Luc. "I'm still nervous of course, but I know that Tommy is in good hands. I'm more concerned about the pain he'll be in afterward, and the physical therapy he'll go through."

Speaking of being nervous...

She and Luc had barely talked since Saturday. What if he'd had enough? Would he back out on their deal and ask her for a divorce?

Of course he wouldn't. But it didn't hurt to prepare herself for the worst. Everyone should have a backup plan.

How could things go from blissful perfection to so unbearably confusing so damned fast?

Julie left briefly to get them lunch from the cafeteria, and when she came back, Amelia was beaming.

"You just missed Luc."

Down her heart went into her stomach again.

"How did it go?" she asked, even though Amelia's relief was explanation enough.

"The surgery was a success and Tommy is in Recovery and doing great."

"That's wonderful news," she said, hugging Amelia. With the surgery over and declared a success, it was time to talk to Luc.

After Tommy had been returned to his room and

settled in, Julie went by Luc's office, almost hoping he wouldn't be there. But he was. He sat at his desk, chair turned toward the window, his back to her, hands folded in his lap.

It took all of her courage to step inside and close the door, and if Luc was aware of her presence, he didn't let on.

"Hey," she said, so nervous that her hands were trembling.

"Hey," he replied, not turning around. Not even moving.

"Can we talk?"

He swiveled around to face her. He wasn't smiling. He wasn't frowning, either. His features looked frozen in a nonexpression, his eyes blank. "About what?"

"This thing happening between us."

"You mean love?"

She cringed.

He shook his head, looking so disappointed. "You can't even stand to hear me say it, can you?"

"It's not that. I just…"

"Don't bother trying to explain. I know you well enough to recognize when you're running away."

She could understand why it might look that way. But she didn't want to *go* anywhere. "I'm not, I swear."

"You just don't trust me."

Why would he think that? After all they had been through. "That's not true."

"Isn't it? Then tell me why you kept your condo?"

She bit her lip, unsure of how to answer, to make him understand.

"Speechless?" he asked. "Always have a backup

plan. Isn't that what you've always told me? I just never imagined you would need a backup plan from me."

To deny it would be a lie. And it sounded horrible when he said it like that.

He leaned forward in his chair. "I know you better than you know yourself, Julie, and maybe that's the problem. I got too close and now you're running scared. You don't trust me."

"I do, it's just… Can't we just go back to the way things were before? When we were best friends?"

He sighed and sagged back into his chair. "We can't unring the bell. And I can't go on pretending that everything is okay. Because it's not."

She felt utterly sick inside. "I don't want to lose you. You mean more to me than anything."

"Just not enough to love me."

He was breaking her heart. "Luc—"

He held his hand up to stop her. "Sorry, that was a low blow. It was uncalled for. Like you said so many times before, you feel what you feel. Or don't feel. And the fact of the matter is that I love you and you don't feel the same about me."

"If we could just talk about this—"

"There's nothing to say. My mind is made up."

Her heart dropped so violently she could barely breathe. It wasn't supposed to be like this. He was supposed to agree with her. He'd always been on her side, but now, when she needed him most, he was just going to do what? Divorce her?

"W-what are you saying?" she asked, her voice so wobbly her words were barely understandable.

"We can't be together anymore," he told her. "Not like before."

"Are you saying you want a divorce?"

"I made you a promise, one I intend to keep. We can go on living like a married couple, but it would be best if we saw each other as little as possible. That will be much easier if you take the spare room downstairs."

She could hardly believe this was happening. He was ending their relationship, just like that? "So that's it? We're not even friends anymore?"

"That's it," he said, that damned blank look on his face. He could have the decency to show a little emotion, to feel angry or hurt. *Something.*

"What about work? Are you firing me?"

"No, but I think that after you establish your citizenship, you should consider looking for another position. It would be easier on everyone."

Then what reason did she even have to stay in Royal? She'd had such grand plans for making Royal her home, and suddenly now they were unraveling around her. Maybe she would be better off in South Africa after all. Maybe it would give her the chance to make a new start.

Julie was a nervous wreck for the next few days, praying she didn't run into Luc, then feeling so cold and empty inside when she didn't. Luc was really good at making himself scarce.

How was it that just a week ago everything was fine. She was happy, he was happy. Why did he have to go and ruin everything?

That wasn't fair and she knew it. This wasn't his fault. It was all her. But she missed him, in a way she had never missed anyone. She woke up lonely and went to bed feeling sick. When she was able to sleep, which wasn't often, he tormented her in her dreams.

He preoccupied her mind until she could barely think of anything else.

What the hell was wrong with her? Why was she such a mess?

She tried her best to keep her feelings to herself, to put on a good face, but she must not have been very convincing because Amelia confronted her Sunday afternoon at the hospital.

Tommy was working with his physical therapist and making impressive progress, so Julie and Amelia went down to the cafeteria for lunch.

"I am not going to miss this hospital food," Amelia said, glaring with contempt at her overcooked burger and soggy fries. Julie pushed her tuna salad around the plate but couldn't make herself take a bite.

"You've been unusually somber this last week," Amelia said.

So much for putting on a good face. She felt like an empty shell, as if losing Luc had sucked everything she loved about life right from her. The days seemed to have no point. Food lost its flavor and not even sleep was an escape from the harsh reality of how horribly she had screwed things up. Why hadn't she just told Luc that she loved him?

Because it would have been a lie, and no matter how much she missed him, he deserved someone who could love him with her whole heart. Someone who trusted him the way she never could.

"I thought I would give you time to work it through before offering an ear," Amelia said, "but we have to leave tomorrow. Could you at least assure me that you're okay?"

Julie put her fork down, feeling hollowed out and cold. A nonperson. "To be honest, I'm not sure if I am."

Amelia's brow knit with concern. "Do you want to talk about it?"

She hadn't intended to tell Amelia about her pretend marriage, but there was no way to explain the situation without telling her the whole truth. Besides, *not* telling her seemed dishonest somehow. "If I tell you a secret, do you promise not to say anything to anyone. And I mean no one."

"Of course."

She took a deep breath and said quietly, so no one else would hear, "Luc and I aren't really a couple. We only got married to keep me from getting deported."

Amelia sat back, looking stunned. "I have a hard time believing that."

"It's the truth."

"You two are Royal's 'it' couple. Everyone talks about you. You're the blueprint for the ideal marriage. The fairy tale come true."

She'd had no idea people viewed her and Luc's marriage that way. It looked as though they had successfully pulled the wool over everyone's eyes. Which only made her feel more depressed and vacant.

"So, if you're just friends, your relationship isn't physical?"

"Well, it was. But not anymore."

"Something happened?"

Unable to even look at her food, Julie pushed her tray away. "He told me that he's in love with me."

Amelia looked confused. "And that's a bad thing?"

"It's not part of the plan."

"The plan? Wow, sounds serious."

"We weren't supposed to fall in love, but he broke the rules and now our friendship is over."

Amelia sat a little straighter. "So, what are you saying—he's available?"

That was a strange question. "I suppose so."

"And you aren't in love with him."

She didn't like the direction this conversation was taking. "I tried. I just can't feel something that I don't."

"You're sure."

Julie blinked. "Of course I'm sure. If I were in love with someone, don't you think I would know it?"

Amelia was quiet for several seconds, mulling something over, her expression serious. "If I tell *you* a secret, do you promise not to tell anyone?"

"Of course."

She looked around and lowered her voice. "This is a little embarrassing, but when I made the decision to come here, I sort of had it in my mind that if Luc was still single, and there was still a spark…"

Julie's heart skipped a beat, then picked up triple time.

"When I thought he was a married man I backed off. But if your marriage is a fake, maybe I should re-think things."

"Maybe you should," Julie agreed.

"That wouldn't bother you? Not even a little? Because now that I know you're not really married, what reason would I have not to go after him myself? It wouldn't technically be cheating."

"No, but—"

"Hell, for all you know, he and I are already fooling around."

She could see what Amelia was doing, and it wasn't going to work. "But you're not."

"How do you know that when he's 'working late' he's not actually with me? I'm at the hospital 24/7 It would be really easy for us to fool around behind your back. Maybe use your condo for a quickie."

"But you wouldn't do that to a friend," Julie said.

"Are you sure? How well do you really know me? Maybe people hate me so much because they've seen Luc and I together. They know we're messing around."

Julie knew Amelia was only trying to make a point, but she felt unsettled nonetheless. "I'm sure someone would have mentioned it."

"You would think so, but all my friends—or should I say ex-friends—knew what Tom was doing and no one said a word to me about it. I didn't find out until after the divorce that he'd had sex with my maid of honor in the men's room at our wedding reception."

Julie gasped. "Did he really?"

"And what about the nurse I saw Luc take into his office the other day after his secretary left? What reason do you think he had to close and lock the door? Maybe you aren't the only friend he's sleeping with."

Julie felt a twinge of something unpleasant. "We are talking hypothetically."

"Are we? If I did see Luc with another woman would you want to know the truth? Would it even matter? If you're not really married—"

"Yes!" Julie said, much louder than she'd intended, causing the people around them to turn and look. She lowered her voice to a whisper. "Yes, I would want to know. And yes, it would matter."

"Why?"

She felt her coffee rising back up her throat.

"You're looking a little pale," Amelia said. "Something eating at you?"

"Is he really seeing someone else?"

"Why does it matter?"

She didn't know why. "It just does."

"Perhaps you're feeling a little jealous?" Amelia said.

Julie's first reaction was to deny it, but whoever the woman was, if there really was another woman, Julie wanted to claw her eyes out.

Oh God, she was jealous. And not just a little. The thought of Luc being intimate with someone besides her made her feel like barfing. "That doesn't mean I'm in love with him."

"Since you became friends, how many serious relationships have either of you been in?" Amelia asked her.

Julie frowned. "Well, I haven't been in any, and if Luc was seeing anyone seriously he never told me. But we're both very focused on our careers. We don't have time for serious relationships."

"Yet you manage to find time for each other."

She was right. Luc had always made time for her and she him. With the exception of the past few days, they'd barely gone twenty-four hours without talking to each other in six years. The day wouldn't feel complete if she didn't hear his voice at least once. And lately, with all the fantastic sex they'd been having…

She thought of him touching another woman the way he touched her, or even just holding another woman's hand, and felt sick inside. Before now she just hadn't let herself think about it. Now she could think of nothing else.

"Oh my God," she said, barely able to catch her breath as reality cracked her hard in the chops. "Oh my God."

She must have started turning blue, because Amelia gave her shoulder a nudge and said, "Breathe, Julie."

She sucked in a deep breath. "Oh my God. I'm in love with Luc."

Amelia was smiling. "Funny how it sneaks up on you."

How had this happened? *When* had it happened? Was she just so used to suppressing her feelings and guarding her heart that she hadn't *allowed* herself to see it?

Now that she had, it was almost overwhelming. She felt happy and excited and scared to death. But in a good way.

"I'm in love with Luc," she said again, the words rolling so naturally off her tongue it was as if they had been there all along, just waiting to be set free. "I. Am in love. With Luc."

In the midst of all those feelings she had another thought, one that sent the air hissing from her balloon of happiness.

"I know what you're thinking," Amelia said, her words startling Julie.

"What am I thinking?"

"You're afraid that it's too late, that you blew it. You're terrified that he's going to reject you."

She'd deny it if she could, but that would be a lie. And hadn't she been lying to herself for long enough? Wasn't it about time that she be honest not just to Luc, but to herself? She'd taken a lot of chances in her life, lived on the edge, but why was she so afraid to take a chance on Luc? And at this point, what did she have to lose?

"I think I need to talk to him," she told Amelia.

"I think you do, too."

Her hands began to shake and her heart went berserk in her chest. "What if it's too late?"

"Then, you can at least say that you tried."

Luc had the courage to put himself out there. To take a chance on her. And for his trouble, all he'd gotten was shot down. Now she needed to do the same for him.

"I have to go," she said. "I have to talk to him."

"Yes you do."

"What time are you leaving tomorrow?"

"As soon as Tommy is discharged. Probably around noon."

"I'll be back to say goodbye." They both stood and Julie hugged her hard. "Thank you so much."

"For what?"

"Making me see what an idiot I am."

"Well, we all act like idiots at one point or another."

If that was the case, Julie was queen of the idiots. She gave Amelia another squeeze, then set off to find Luc, hoping she wasn't too late.

"Are you going to mope around all day?"

Luc looked up from his computer screen, which he hadn't bothered to turn on yet, to find his mother in the doorway of his home office. "I'm not moping. I'm reflecting."

"She'll come around."

He hadn't said a word to his mother about the Julie situation, so either Julie had told her or she'd figured it out on her own.

He'd honestly believed that giving Julie an ultimatum, threatening their friendship, would make her see reason. Five days later he was still waiting.

Talk about a major fail.

Now he'd painted himself into a corner and he wasn't sure how to get back out. If this time apart had proved anything, it was how much he needed her in his life. Even if all she could be to him was a friend. He'd screwed up big-time and now he had to figure out a way to make it right. If that was even a viable option at this point. He had failed Julie in the worst possible way. She needed to know that he was there for her no matter what; instead he'd given up on her. He couldn't imagine a worse betrayal.

"I don't suppose you've seen Houdini."

Luc gestured behind him, to the window valance, where the kitten sat a good eight feet off the ground, happy as could be. Despite being blind, or maybe because of it, he was fearless. In the past few days he'd taken full run of the house, where there were virtually millions of places to disappear. But on the bright side, he was starting to learn his name, and would sometimes come when called. If all else failed, opening a can of cat food usually did the trick.

"Is there anything I can do?" his mother asked, and Luc shook his head. "I just hate to see you both so unhappy."

He swiveled his chair around and looked out the window. It was nearly April and the spring flowers were in full bloom. Yet he'd never felt more depressed and gloomy. "She made her choice."

She sighed. "You're making this so much more complicated than it has to be."

That was easy for her to say.

"She's right, you know."

At the sound of Julie's voice, he swiveled back around. She stood in the doorway behind his mother.

"Would you look at the time," his mother said, wheeling herself out the door. "I'm late for my physical therapy."

"Can we talk?" Julie asked him. She looked almost as bad as he felt. Her voice quivered and he could see that her hands were trembling. What now? Was she going to ask him for a divorce? Put an end to this charade before they caused any more damage?

"I guess that depends what you have to say."

"You can't even imagine how hard this is for me. Letting my guard down. Admitting how wrong I was. I screwed up. I was too scared to admit how I was really feeling. I couldn't even admit it to myself."

"And how are you *really* feeling?"

"I love you. I'm *in love* with you. This week apart has been awful."

He didn't want to appear too eager. After all, he did still have his pride to consider. But he was having a whole lot of trouble keeping his butt in the chair. He needed her in his arms. Needed to smell her hair and taste her lips. He just plain needed her.

Her voice shook when she said, "I know it's a lot to ask, and I probably don't deserve it, but if you could give me just one more chance."

"You're right, it is a lot to ask," he said. And if he didn't love her so much, he may have told her to take a hike. Luckily for them both, he just couldn't seem to live without her. "How do I know that you won't freak out and change your mind?"

"You don't know. And I have no clue how to convince you, if that's even possible. But I had to try."

He rose from his chair and though Julie looked terrified, she stood her ground. He walked over to her, until they were nearly toe to toe, and said, "We could start with a hug, and go from there."

He could see the instant she finally let go. The defenses dropped and she threw her arms around him, a quivering bundle. "I'm so sorry," she said.

He held her tight. This was right where she belonged. With him, forever. He wouldn't be letting her go again. "I'm the one who's sorry. My pride was bruised. I never should have given up on you."

She sighed, laying her cheek against his shirt. "You had to. It was the kick in the pants that I needed."

He cradled her face in his hands. There were tears in her eyes, but they were happy. "I love you, Julie."

"I love you, too," she said, "So much. I can't believe I almost blew it."

He grinned down at her, so relieved and happy it almost didn't seem real. "You didn't. I wouldn't have given up so easily."

"Amelia told me that everyone considers you and I the blueprint for the perfect marriage. The fairy tale come true."

"I guess they were right," he said.

"But we still have one thing left to do," she told him. "To make it official."

"What's that?"

She smiled and kissed him, with so much love in her eyes it almost hurt. "Live happily ever after."

* * * * *

TEXAS CATTLEMAN'S CLUB: AFTER THE STORM
Don't miss a single story!

STRANDED WITH THE RANCHER
by Janice Maynard
SHELTERED BY THE MILLIONAIRE
by Catherine Mann
PREGNANT BY THE TEXAN
by Sara Orwig
BECAUSE OF THE BABY...
by Cat Schield
HIS LOST AND FOUND FAMILY
by Sarah M. Anderson
MORE THAN A CONVENIENT BRIDE
by Michelle Celmer
FOR HIS BROTHER'S WIFE
by Kathie DeNosky

If you're on Twitter, tell us what you think of
Harlequin Desire! #harlequindesire

REQUEST YOUR FREE BOOKS!
2 FREE NOVELS PLUS 2 FREE GIFTS!

HARLEQUIN® *Desire*

ALWAYS POWERFUL, PASSIONATE AND PROVOCATIVE

YES! Please send me 2 FREE Harlequin Desire® novels and my 2 FREE gifts (gifts are worth about $10). After receiving them, if I don't wish to receive any more books, I can return the shipping statement marked "cancel." If I don't cancel, I will receive 6 brand-new novels every month and be billed just $4.55 per book in the U.S. or $4.99 per book in Canada. That's a savings of at least 13% off the cover price! It's quite a bargain! Shipping and handling is just 50¢ per book in the U.S. and 75¢ per book in Canada.* I understand that accepting the 2 free books and gifts places me under no obligation to buy anything. I can always return a shipment and cancel at any time. Even if I never buy another book, the two free books and gifts are mine to keep forever.

225/326 HDN F4ZC

Name _____ (PLEASE PRINT) _____

Address _____ Apt. #

City _____ State/Prov. _____ Zip/Postal Code

Signature (if under 18, a parent or guardian must sign)

Mail to the **Harlequin® Reader Service:**
IN U.S.A.: P.O. Box 1867, Buffalo, NY 14240-1867
IN CANADA: P.O. Box 609, Fort Erie, Ontario L2A 5X3

Want to try two free books from another line?
Call 1-800-873-8635 or visit www.ReaderService.com.

* Terms and prices subject to change without notice. Prices do not include applicable taxes. Sales tax applicable in N.Y. Canadian residents will be charged applicable taxes. Offer not valid in Quebec. This offer is limited to one order per household. Not valid for current subscribers to Harlequin Desire books. All orders subject to credit approval. Credit or debit balances in a customer's account(s) may be offset by any other outstanding balance owed by or to the customer. Please allow 4 to 6 weeks for delivery. Offer available while quantities last.

Your Privacy—The Harlequin® Reader Service is committed to protecting your privacy. Our Privacy Policy is available online at www.ReaderService.com or upon request from the Harlequin Reader Service.

We make a portion of our mailing list available to reputable third parties that offer products we believe may interest you. If you prefer that we not exchange your name with third parties, or if you wish to clarify or modify your communication preferences, please visit us at www.ReaderService.com/consumerschoice or write to us at Harlequin Reader Service Preference Service, P.O. Box 9062, Buffalo, NY 14269. Include your complete name and address.

HD13R

Without warning, Gavin stood up. Suddenly the office shrank in size. His personality and masculine presence sucked up all the available oxygen. Pacing so near Cassidy's chair that he almost brushed her knees, Gavin shot her a look laden with frustration. "We need some ground rules if you're going to stay with me while we sort out this pregnancy, Cassidy. First of all, we're going to forget that we've ever seen each other naked."

She gulped, fixating on the dusting of hair where the shallow V-neck of his sweater revealed a peek of his chest. "I'm pretty sure that's going to be the elephant in the room. Our night in Vegas was amazing. Maybe not for you, but for me. Telling me to forget it is next to impossible."

"Good Lord, woman. Don't you have any social armor, at all?"

"I am not a liar. If you want me to pretend we haven't been intimate, I'll try, but I make no promises."

He leaned over her, resting his hands on the arms of the chair. His beautifully sculpted lips were in kissing distance. Smoke-colored irises filled with turbulent emotions locked on hers like lasers. "I may be attracted to you, Cass, but I don't completely trust you. It's too soon. So, despite evidence to the contrary, I do have some self-control."

Maybe *he* did, but hers was melting like snow in the hot sun. His coffee-scented breath brushed her cheek. This close, she could see tiny crinkles at the corners of his eyes. She might have called them laugh lines if she could imagine her onetime lover being lighthearted enough and smiling long enough to create them.

"You're crowding my personal space," she said primly.

For several seconds, she was sure he was going to steal a kiss. Her breathing went shallow, her nipples tightened and a tumultuous feeling rose in her chest. Something volatile. For the first time, she understood that whatever madness had taken hold of them in Las Vegas was neither a fluke nor a solitary event.

Don't miss
TWINS ON THE WAY
by USA TODAY *bestselling author Janice Maynard.*

Available April 2015,
wherever Harlequin® Desire books and ebooks are sold.

www.Harlequin.com

HARLEQUIN®

A *Romance* FOR EVERY MOOD™

JUST CAN'T GET ENOUGH?

Join our social communities
and talk to us online.

You will have access to the latest
news on upcoming titles and special
promotions, but most importantly,
you can talk to other fans about your
favorite Harlequin reads.

Harlequin.com/Community

f Facebook.com/HarlequinBooks

Twitter.com/HarlequinBooks

P Pinterest.com/HarlequinBooks

HARLEQUIN®

A *Romance* FOR EVERY MOOD™

**Stay up-to-date on all your
romance-reading news with the
Harlequin Shopping Guide,
featuring bestselling authors, exciting new
miniseries, books to watch and more!**

The newest issue will be delivered right to you
with our compliments! There are 4 each year.

Signing up is easy.

EMAIL

ShoppingGuide@Harlequin.ca

WRITE TO US

HARLEQUIN BOOKS
Attention: Customer Service Department
P.O. Box 9057, Buffalo, NY 14269-9057

OR PHONE

1-800-873-8635 in the United States
1-888-343-9777 in Canada

Please allow 4-6 weeks for delivery of the first issue by mail.